Underland Arcana explores the parts of our heart which we don't want to share with others. Stories about spending time with family, stories about finding your way back to family, stories about the terrible secrets families keep, and stories about what happens when families rot from within. Why, yes, this issue is all about those connections that sustain and inflame us.

© 2022 Firebird Creative LLC and the respective contributors.

Underland Arcana is published quarterly. This issue is published in conjunction with the new moon that slips across the edge of the world and creeps across a new sky.

EDITOR
Mark Teppo

COVER IMAGE
DGIM Studios

SIGIL ART
Andrew Penn Romine

PUBLISHER
Underland Press
Clackamas, OR, USA

And then, in the night, drifting on the waves . . .

https://www.underlandarcana.com

UNDERLAND ARCANA

~ 06 ~

Underland Press

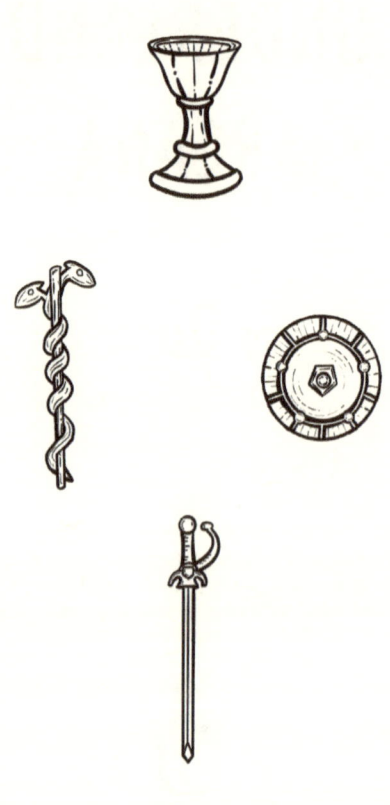

Contents

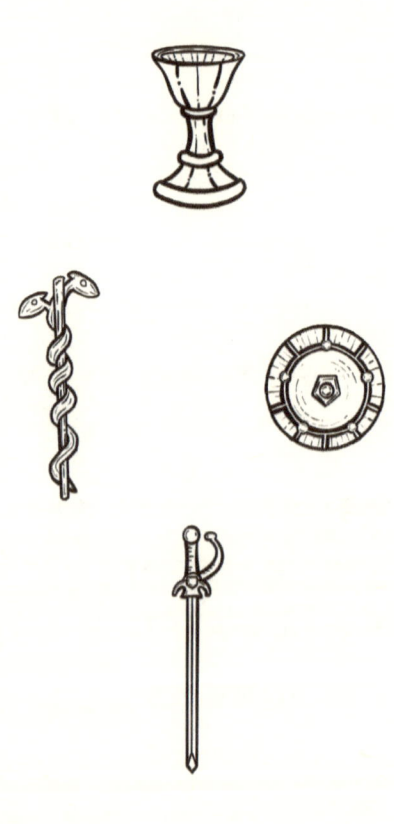

The Revelation of the Fish

This is the fish issue. This issue is the one that isn't like the others, though I probably say that about each of them. But this one—this one, specifically—is the one where I went this way instead of that way when it came to the cover.

I had done a year or so of skulls. Skulls and scary faces. It's a motif of the first year; I will admit to that now, looking back. But when I was considering the cover for issue 6, I had a moment when I was messing around with ideas and there it was: the fish cover. It wasn't like any of the others. I hesitated, overthought it, and then went for a second opinion.

The second opinion loved it, and I thought, "Okay, well, I pretend that was the plan all along." (Dear reader: it wasn't.) And this fortuitous moment—this giving myself up to the creative spirit and letting it guide me— marks a shift in the tone for *Arcana*. In true hindsight (in, say, 2025, when I am totally not retconning some of these editorials for the relaunch of *Arcana*—shhh!), it's this cover that marks that change. The *fish* cover.

(And while I'm admitting to telling this story about my mindset in 2022 from 2025, I'll note the progression that follows: fish again with 7, the deer lady with 8, and the well-dressed rabbit for 9. There is WTF? Whimsy here, and I'm glad it surfaced. These four covers are my favorites. 10 is a homage to a very important source of inspiration for all of this, and 11 is a return of the skull motif. And yeah, so is 12, actually, but let's not confuse everything too much by talking about the future while doing revision on the past.)

Anyway, here are some stories to ease us into spring. May we all have a chance to go outside and find each other again.

Mark Teppo
April 12th, 2022

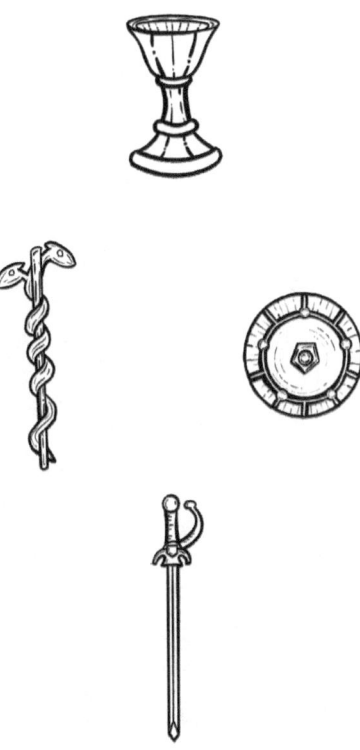

QUEEN of SWORDS.

I See You

~ *Gerri Leen*

I look, tasting the moment, the hesitation—even perhaps the fear—as you take me in with a sideways "I might not have seen you" glance. Will you run? Leave the bar and go find your girl of the moment in some other place? I know you won't look me straight in the eye.

Even that night you didn't. When we touched, the lights were out, my hair whipping around your face but our features hazy at best.

That was great.

I could have been anyone.

You're great.

I am. Not that you'd know it.

I have an early meeting. I know this is . . . awkward. But I really need to get my rest and I sleep best alone.

So cold. You could have been made of stone.

I left, like a dutiful doormat. Used and discarded. Hurting because I thought you liked me.

I make my way to where you are. I don't look directly at you, either, but I'm like a hunting cat, keeping you in my sights even as I pretend to have other prey in mind.

God, you're beautiful.

But how did you know? You never even saw me there.

Not the woman I am. All you wanted was the body that you took fast and hard, not seeming to think you should make it good for me too.

You edge toward the bar, and I move to block your way to the door, just in case you lose your nerve and try to flee. But you don't.

I should give you credit for that. You stride forth to a stool like some mythical hero. Your phone your shield, your wallet full of cash your sword. Women will fall before you like soldiers to a superior force.

The one you've picked for the night is already yielding—you have a type, don't you? Those of us who want but can't have, who sit and wait as our fairer sisters are taken to the dance floor, offered drinks, seduced onto balconies and decks and into grimy bathroom stalls.

We are the left behinds, the uncomfortable, the fidgeters, the ones who wonder why we picked this dress, these shoes, this purse that's too big to put on the bar and too little to put at our feet.

I came without a purse this time. I came not in a slinky dress but jeans and a leather jacket. My boots are flat and sensible and could kick you to shit.

My hair is curly tonight. I didn't spend hours trying to tame the whirls and serpentine bits that refuse to give in to the flat iron and blow dryer without a fight.

Under my jacket, I have on a plain white t-shirt. In my pocket I have my phone, my keys, my lip balm, and enough money to buy my own damn drinks.

I am not here to catch. I am here to set free.

The woman you've latched onto looks at me. She's annoyed. This is her moment—possibly the only one that will come—and I'm ruining it.

I nod to you, noticing you still won't turn to face me fully. I call you by the wrong name. It's petty but it amuses me, and your face twists in what looks like irritation.

She doesn't frown. You haven't gotten to the introduction stage yet. For all she knows, that is your name.

I lean in and smell her perfume. Desperate and exactly what I wore the other night. We are all twins, in our sleek outfits with our self-tanned legs and straight hair and spicy floral scent.

Tonight, I wear lemon. It reminds me of youth, of a time when men did not slay me after I gave them everything.

I tip her chin up, turning gently, making her look from you to me. Her skin is soft—too soft for the likes of you. "He's selfish and he won't make you come. He'll send you home once he's finished with you. Come find me when it's done. We'll be a gang, sisters tarnished by this man's blade." I make a sneering noise. "Well, not that large a blade, if we're being honest—just between us girls."

You try to pull her away.

You're special. I could see that right away.

You weren't wrong. You also weren't sincere. Special to you means victim, means prey, means strike fast then leave. Means cut out my heart. Why not take my hands too? My head?

You can take what you want—no matter how deep the cut, you won't kill what's real inside me. You won't slay the monster you've awakened.

"He hurt you," the woman says.

I nod. "He'll hurt you, too. But if you need to go down that road, do it. Sometime pain is liberating."

She looks rebellious. Like she doesn't believe me—or doesn't want to. For women like us, those are often the same thing.

And you want her. It's a powerful thing for a girl who's usually left sitting, guarding the drinks.

"She's just pissed it didn't work out for us." Your voice is soft, reasonable even. Using logic in the face of my bitterness. Mister Rational.

I can see immediately that it's the wrong tack to take. She looks at you, her head cocked, her eyes almost fiery in the low light. "How long were you together?"

How long did you give it? That's what she's asking and she already knows the answer—she's figured it out. She's smarter than I was. But then I didn't have me telling me hard truths.

I smirk. You stare into the mirror over the bar and our eyes finally meet.

You're not as handsome as I remember. Not now that I see you fully, with eyes not blinded by relief, by gratitude, by loneliness. You have a weak chin. Shifty eyes. And you're sweating.

I let one side of my mouth go up slowly, the universal sign of contempt. I know my eyes are dead.

She's the one who responds. She laughs and slides off the barstool. "You look so cool," she says to me. "Wild. Sexy."

Everything I thought you were.

I don't take my eyes from yours. You stand frozen, your mouth grim.

"I am. You can be, too." I finally break the gaze and take her hand, pulling her onto the dance floor. Our dance isn't sexual. It's defiance. It's victory.

Men stop to watch, frozen. As if they've never seen two women dance for themselves, not for them.

"My friends are freaking," she says with a laugh. "They always leave me behind but now I'm getting all the attention."

"No one leaves us behind anymore."

Her smile falters. Her "that's right" is shaky. There's something lost about her, as if suddenly she's doubting our path.

I slip my jacket off and put it around her. It's heavy and warm and broken in perfectly. She's smaller than I am so it swallows her a little. I tell her it suits her and it does. I'm not going to lie about things like that. We don't need that.

Then a new woman comes into the bar. She sees you, her face broken—but her back straight.

"Sister," I whisper, recognizing another former lost soul, and take the hand of my new friend.

We follow the girl as she strides to the bar—to you.

She's in black jeans. A gray tank top. Sneakers and a bracelet of skulls around her wrist.

You see her in the mirror, then you see us. You don't move except to motion for the bartender as if we're nothing to you. Just three women happening to stand behind you—not a threat, not a reminder, not revenge waiting to happen.

You can pretend all you want, but the way your hand shakes as you lift the glass to your mouth lets us know what you're really feeling.

I reach the new woman just before she gets to you. "There's no satisfaction there."

She turns to face me. She's prettier than my new friend and I are. You threw her away too? Do none of us measure up for you?

"This is our bar now," I say. My new friend nods. This pretty girl turns and stares at you in the mirror.

You glance up, frozen, not a single forgivable excuse coming from you. Not a lie, either. Or an insult. You say nothing.

Stone cold silent.

But men like you always are. Even when you never shut up.

Me? I feel like anything but stone. It's as if there's a fire inside me. I grab my girls' hands and lead them to the other side of the bar. We're proud, even if we're just learning to be. We're beautiful, even if we aren't. We're not seat-holders. We're not the girls who wait.

We soon have men hovering. We don't have to pay for our own drinks.

We do anyway.

PAGE of SWORDS.

Filtration Systems

~ Mary Berman

On the day Jimmy Tomlinson murdered 98.96% of the population of Garbersdale, the sky was bright and cloudless.

It happened at eleven o'clock in the morning. He should have been in school with the other teenagers, but he was the sort of boy who was always trying to wrangle his way out of school, and his parents were the sort of parents who let him. So, at ten fifty-eight on the day he killed everybody, he was sitting in his room with a pair of earbuds in, playing with a computer program he had developed.

The program was designed to synthesize the most unpleasant sounds possible. While developing it Jimmy had also been modifying an industrial speaker system he'd bought off Craigslist. The Craigslist ad had said that when the speakers were turned up to full volume, their sound could be heard across three city blocks. Jimmy was trying to modify them so they could be heard across the whole town.

He'd explained this two weeks ago to Orla Harrisburg, who had come over insisting that she only wanted to work on their group calculus project—but when she agreed to come up to his room, he knew she was into him. He played her a little of his sound sequence—only a little, because it wasn't yet half as offensive as he knew it could be—and described, while his blood throbbed, his plan use both in conjunction to terrorize the town.

Orla eyed the speaker, which occupied an entire wall of Jimmy's room. It hulked like a slab of volcanic rock. "That's it?"

". . . Yeah." What did she mean, *That's it?* He was a genius.

"Why would you do something like that?" Orla asked.

"Come on. I hate this place. Don't you?"

"No," said Orla matter-of-factly. "And it seems like an awful lot of work. Why d'you hate everything so much?"

The compact seed of anger that had been rooted in Jimmy's guts for as long as he could remember put forth another sprout. Its tendrils crawled up his stomach wall and knotted about his trachea. "Fuck you," he said. "Let's work on the project."

Orla had stiffened. Then she'd informed him that she would prefer to work on the project herself, and she'd removed her smooth slim limbs from his bedroom.

Two weeks later Jimmy was still brooding over the incident, simmering away in front of his computer, thinking: How could Orla ask him something like that? He was just angry, that was all. And that day, the way Orla had looked at him as though he were malformed—*she* was the one who'd made him angry. It was her fault. His parents and his teachers and everyone else who insisted that he do things he didn't want to do, it was their fault. Even strangers he encountered in the grocery store or at the coffee shop or the movie theater, strangers who persisted in being idiots or assholes or ugly or rude: their fault. In response to such a high volume of fucking *people*, it was perfectly normal to be angry.

So thick vines of anger had kept strangling Jimmy's organs, and he had kept on working on his synthesizer.

And now, at ten fifty-nine on Wednesday morning, he yanked his earbuds out, leaned over and vomited into the wastebasket.

Jimmy caught his breath. His heart juddered arrhythmically. In fact, he was pretty sure it had actually stopped for a second. The noise had been so ugly, so dissonant, so *wrong* that it had made him physically ill. But even as he sat there, his stomach still twisted, wiping a string of vomit and saliva from his chin, he felt a bold flicker of grim joy. He grinned. *This* would mess everyone up all right. This would show Orla. He unplugged his earbuds, plugged in the speaker, and hit Play.

The sound slammed into his eardrums like a sledgehammer; like an undersea volcano, cracking the planet and displacing unfathomable tons of ocean; like an asteroid smacking off a hunk of the moon.

Jimmy keeled over instantly. So did his father, who was working from home, and his mother, at a deli half a mile away. So did virtually everyone else within a three-quarter-mile radius, including almost the full population of Garbersdale, plus a hundred or so people in the neighboring towns of Peterborough, Mixton, and Shell's Way.

But this story isn't about Jimmy Tomlinson.

☉

At eleven o'clock exactly, everyone else in Jisoo Kim's eighth grade algebra class toppled out of their desks and hit the linoleum.

Jisoo blinked. Her chest tightened. This was another one of those jokes no one had thought to let her in on, because it had spread by whisper and Jisoo, being deaf, could not hear whispers. This sort of thing happened all the time, and Jisoo tried not to let on how much it hurt her. She knew her friends and peers meant nothing by it, they just forgot, but, well. She smiled weakly, trying to seem cool and casual and happy, wondering if it was too late for her to fall out of her chair and participate as well. Then she realized that the teacher was also prostrate, and that Ricky Carlsson, who had been leaning over precariously to pass Paul Tiny a note, had crumpled and landed on the crown of his head, and his neck was now twisted at a brutal angle, and no one was doing anything about it. And then she noticed that no one's chest was moving.

A dull rhythmic vibration pulsed beatlike through the soles of her shoes.

"Guys?" she said. No one reacted. Her own chest tightened further; her heart began to hammer in a way it had never done before, her blood becoming more tangible beat by beat against the inside of her skin. She stood up, hesitated, and then, convinced that this was a joke on her but too anxious to care, touched Kelly Martin's neck. There was no pulse.

"Oh my god," Jisoo said. She staggered back and whammed her hip into a desk. "Oh my god oh my g–"

She fled the classroom, her hands over her mouth, careening through the halls to the nurse's office. She burst in, already babbling, "I think everyone's dead, I really think everyone's dead," and then stopped. A noise that wanted to be a scream clawed halfway up her throat and lodged there. The student aide had collapsed face-down on his keyboard. The two kids who'd been sitting in the waiting room lolled in the pea-green chairs, their eyes vacant and their mouths open.

Jisoo ran into one of the little private rooms with bunk beds and jugs of water, still searching for the nurse. She didn't find him, but she did find Allie Petrovsky from world history class. Allie was lying on her back with a pair of noise-canceling headphones on and her eyes shut. She hadn't responded to Jisoo barreling in, but she did appear to be breathing. Jisoo said her name. Allie didn't move. Jisoo went over and shook her.

Allie jumped and opened her eyes. "Jisoo?" she said, which was easy to read. "What?"

Jisoo was so relieved she burst into tears.

She flung her arms around Allie, squeezing her so tightly that Allie couldn't even reach up to take her headphones off. Jisoo could feel the vibrations of Allie talking, but she couldn't bring herself to let go long enough to look at Allie's mouth. She became conscious of movement behind her and turned. Two girls were standing in the doorway: Carla White, looking even blanker than usual, and Laila Siddique, wearing her sensitivity suit and shaking her head like she was trying to get rid of a mosquito.

Jisoo screamed, mostly from delight, and cried harder.

"Hey, chill out," Laila said. "What's going on?" She rubbed her ears, crinkling the cellophane-like fabric of her suit. Laila had a hypersensitivity disorder, and experiencing the world unfiltered frequently sent her into convulsions, so she wore a full-body sensitivity suit, which stretched over her skin and nostrils and ears and eye sockets and mouth, letting her breathe but dulling all sensory stimuli. Jisoo had used to wonder how she ate lunch, and then she'd watched Laila in the cafeteria one day and realized that Laila did not eat lunch. Eventually she learned that Laila only ate two meals a day, breakfast and dinner, and that she ate them at home in a special room, gray-painted and dimly lit and silent. This made Jisoo sad, and as a consequence seeing Laila usually made her sad, but now Jisoo had never been so happy to see anyone.

"Everyone in Mr. Russo's class just—fell over dead," Jisoo said. She was aware of how absurd she sounded, but her body was too hysterical for her to disbelieve herself. She was still clutching Allie, which was ridiculous. She and Allie weren't even friends. "They're dead out there in the nurse's office, too. Look."

"It's that sound," said Carla dully.

"What sound?"

Allie said something too and reached up to take her headphones off.

"Don't do that," Carla said.

Allie said something else, which Jisoo missed as she turned to her, and removed her headphones. Immediately her eyes rolled back in her head, her mouth fell open, and she flopped sideways into Jisoo's lap. Jisoo screamed again.

Carla ignored her and said to Laila, "Don't take that off."

Laila rubbed her ears again. She'd been sitting in one of the private bunk rooms with Carla, who'd escorted her here for period cramps, when five minutes ago a loud ugly noise had started buzzing its way through her suit. Between that and her knotted stomach and Carla's weird trademark brand of silence, she was feeling irritable. "Why would I take it off?" she snapped. "And what's wrong with Allie? Where's the nurse?" She shook her head hard. "Ugh! What is that!"

"You can hear it?"

"That horrible buzzing? Yes. You're lucky," said Laila to Jisoo, who did not notice.

"Hmm. Your suit must be filtering out whatever frequency is killing people," Carla said. "That's why you're not dead."

"Yeah?" said Laila, humoring her. "Then why aren't you dead? Seriously, what's going on? Allie, get up. You're freaking me out."

"She can't get up. She's dead. Come on." Carla tugged Jisoo out from under Allie Petrovsky. Allie slid off Jisoo and thunked to the floor like a rag doll. "Come on," Carla said, with, for the first time, a touch of real feeling. But Jisoo only drew a deep, shattered breath, and Carla, evidently fed up now, dragged Jisoo out of the room. Laila followed them as far as the nurse's office and then paused to gawk at the two limp, unblinking sixth-graders in the pea-green chairs. She hadn't really noticed them when following Carla to Allie's bunk room. She'd glimpsed them out of the corner of her eye, but the suit tended to blur her peripheral vision, and she'd just assumed they were asleep. But their eyes were open.

It couldn't be true that everyone was dead.

The sixth-graders sure *looked* dead.

"Carla?" Laila said uncomfortably. There was no answer. Laila felt a burst of quiet panic, looked out the door and realized Carla and Jisoo were already halfway down the corridor. She hurried to catch up. "Hey! Wait! What are you doing?"

"We've got to figure out where the sound is coming from and turn it off."

"Shouldn't we call the police? Or our parents?"

"I wouldn't."

"Why not?"

"Well, if they're within range of the sound, they're probably dead like everyone else." A bolt of horror shot through Laila's solar plexus. "And if they're not, you don't want them to hear it, do you?"

Laila's parents both worked in the city, twenty miles away. How far away could the sound be heard? Surely not that far; Laila couldn't even hear it properly. But she had her suit, and her parents.... Her mind wrenched away from the mental image of her parents lolling in their desk chairs with the sixth-graders' limp necks and dead eyes, flitted frantically around her skull for something else to attach to, and latched squidlike onto the police. Laila would call the police. It was what you were supposed to do.

She informed Carla of this. Carla said nothing.

Stubbornly Laila got out her cell phone and called 9-1-1, but when she was halfway through telling the operator their location (they were walking through the cafeteria now, and the kids who'd been eating had collapsed into their trays and lunchboxes, and the cafeteria monitors were prone on the ground, and something in the kitchen was smoking badly), the operator interrupted, sounding first vexed and then nauseous,

"You're not at school. I can hear something in the background. Are you at a concert? Oh, excuse m–" The operator's voice cut off abruptly. Laila heard retching.

The girls entered the empty gym. Briefly, blessedly, the vibrations and buzzing softened, and the echoes of their footsteps against the rubber floor and steel bleachers sounded, muffled, in Laila's ears. Of course, the gym was soundproofed. But it was a lunch period. No one had P.E. during lunch periods, because of recess.

"Hello?" Laila said to the operator. "Hello?" No answer. More retching, then dead air, and then a busy signal that never ended.

Carla pushed open the exit door behind the gym, which led to the street-facing schoolyard. In the same flat tone as always, she asked, "How did that go?"

Laila's thoughts detached from the police and suctioned back onto her parents. Her father's jaw open, his tongue swelling and blackening, her mother's shriveling skin and eyeballs being gnawed away by maggots. "Shut up," she said. She wanted nothing more than to call her mother; she wanted it in her liver, in her fingertips, in the space behind her eyes where she sometimes got migraines. Instead she hung up and, swallowing hard, followed Carla and Jisoo outside.

There was a vicious pile-up in the street. Ten, fifteen, twenty cars had all slammed into each other. Some had spilled over onto the wide flat grassy schoolyard. The day was cloudless and warm, the sky a deep impenetrable blue, and for a split second, as Laila looked at the wreckage and her two classmates and the hot yellow sunlight on the grass, she felt keenly and simultaneously the horror of the death and violence before her, her sick suppressed anxiety, and the pure unfiltered delight of skipping fourth period and sneaking outside on a beautiful day. Then she felt confused, and then she saw a severed head in the middle of the street, and then, much to her own surprise, her legs gave out from under her and she landed in a sitting position on the grass.

Jisoo did not fall. Indeed she looked too paralyzed to fall or throw up or do any of the things Laila's body was insisting ought to be done, too paralyzed to do anything but cling to Carla, who, for her part, had stopped moving. Carla squinted at the wreckage for a second, glanced left toward Main Street, and then turned her attention the other way toward Hopkins Avenue, which marked the start of a residential neighborhood.

Laila asked, "What are you looking for?"

"The source of the sound. I think it has to be close, but I can't tell . . ."

Laila considered. In just six hours her parents would be on their way back to Garbersdale. The fingers of her left hand drifted to those of her right; she hesitated, gulping; then in one swoop she peeled off the right-hand glove of her sensitivity suit and pressed her palm to the ground. The sound's vibrations thudded through her like ocean waves, like honeybee swarms. They were coming from some place past Hopkins. Her body hummed violently. Laila shuddered once, already feeling unglued, and ripped her hand away.

Carla and Jisoo were looking at her. Laila managed to say, "That way."

"Oh," said Carla, respectfully. "That's neat. Come on, then." She took Jisoo's hand and started walking. Laila stayed on the ground for a few more seconds, focusing on the soft, distant sensation of her suit's fabric against her palms, her cheeks and forehead, the insides of her thighs. Then she took a deep, helpless breath, got to her wobbly feet and followed.

They walked toward Hopkins Avenue and turned right on Estaugh Street: Carla marching, Jisoo stumbling, Laila just kind of drifting. They saw two more car accidents, but these weren't as bad, just a pair of crumpled skewed cars with unbroken seatbelted bodies drooping behind their steering wheels. They passed seventeen dead squirrels, at least thirty-two dead songbirds (Laila lost count), two dogs, and a single housecat on its side, fluffy and unmoving. The birds were mostly robins and blue jays and goldfinches and looked like jewels. A man in camouflage-green clothes lay next to a still-running lawnmower, which chewed away placidly at his left foot, slowly turning the fresh-chopped grass a soft rust color. From one house floated the sweet strains of a recorded Bach prelude.

Then, at the same time, Laila and Jisoo stopped. Both girls clapped their hands over their ears and fell back. Jisoo looked astonished. She exclaimed, "I can hear it!"

Carla looked stricken. "I thought you were deaf."

"I am. I mean, I can only hear sounds if they're really intense, which, you know, they're not, usually. But..." Cautiously, she lowered her hands and stepped forward again, an expression of dim wonder on her face.

"No," Carla shouted, but it was too late. Jisoo's eyeballs jittered in her head. She sucked in a strangled breath and fell. Laila lunged forward to grab her and heard, as she had a split second ago, the not-too-muffled strains of a hideous cacophony; she felt her own heart cease to beat and leapt back, out of range, with a gasp. Carla hauled Jisoo over her shoulders and dumped her next to Laila, and Laila crouched over her, stunned and hopeless, feeling for a pulse.

Miraculously, she found one. Jisoo had been moved out of range of the sound before her body had had time to fully shut down. Laila pounded on Jisoo's chest, more so she could feel useful than anything else, and Jisoo inhaled a shallow breath.

Carla covered her face. "That was my fault."

"What?"

"I should've known your filter wouldn't work if you got close enough. And Jisoo . . . Just stay here, okay? I'll find the noise and make it stop. Maybe everyone else will wake up, too, if it stops."

Hysteria bubbled in Laila's chest. "They're not asleep! There's a guy back there missing his head!"

Carla took one step away from her, two, three, then turned on her heel and speedwalked down the street.

"Carla!" Laila bellowed. "Why aren't you dead!"

Carla did not respond, did not even indicate that she'd heard. She broke into a jog, then a run, getting farther and farther away. When she was almost at the end of the street, she slowed down and cocked her head. Then she turned, marched up the porch of a two-story mint-green colonial, hesitated for the briefest second, opened the screen door and walked in.

Carla had spent her entire life screaming.

She didn't remember her first scream or her birth, but she knew from stories that it had involved an emergency C-section. She'd come into the world three months early, horrified by the loud sounds and the bright lights and the big ugly faces. She'd started screaming right away.

She'd screamed incessantly. She would not stop until she fell asleep or ran out of air, and even in the latter case her mouth would stay open, a tiny void, her little throat bobbing in an attempt to scream without breath. She refused to stop screaming long enough to eat or drink. For years she received her nutrition through IV supplements and a gastrointestinal tube. Her parents had not known what to do. She'd kept it up through toddlerhood and young childhood, despite doctors and therapies. She had not been able to go to school or day care; she had been kept home as much as possible, and when it was necessary to bring her somewhere—to run an errand, or to visit relatives—her parents hustled through the task as quickly as possible or left her in the car. Sometimes her father yelled at her to shut up, and sometimes he hit her, but neither act had any noticeable effect.

Her memories of this early screaming were tied up in her other childhood memories, like when the family had visited Carla's aunt in New York and they'd ridden the subway, and a big man with a cane had tripped and fallen and smashed his face open on the subway floor, and Carla had watched his blood, dotted with little grains of broken teeth, slosh up and down with the movement of the train. Her second memory was of watching a mailman on a bicycle get hit by a truck and flattened, spread out over the blacktop like peanut butter. Her third memory was a cloudy one of her family being forced out of their house, sleeping under a bridge in the city for two days, immersed in cold and wet and anxiety before finally moving in with her maternal grandmother in Garbersdale. Then came a series of disjointed memories of her parents fighting, not the way people fight when they're exhausted and frustrated but the way they fight when they hate each other, until eventually her mother got a job and then a promotion and then started making some real money. Carla's next isolated memory, a little later, from age four maybe, was of watching a gas station explode. The fire had consumed six cars, an attached convenience store, and all of the human beings in the vicinity. It had smelled of gasoline and blackened marshmallows. And Carla had screamed right through all of it.

Then, at age five, she'd stopped.

Her parents and doctors never knew why, but the answer was simple: Carla had realized that it did not matter whether she screamed out loud, as long as she was doing it in her head.

In this way she had drowned out every ugly stimulus, every harsh noise, every unwelcome thought. She was now thirteen years old and capable of blocking out anything. In fact, she was incapable of ceasing to block things out. When she and Laila and Jisoo had stepped from the school into the sunlight, she had not experienced Laila's flash of bewildered joy, because she had not noticed the lovely silence and the sun.

She had learned to function through the screaming. She layered it on top of the rest of the world, filtered everything through it. Indeed, if she thought about it, her screaming functioned not unlike Laila's sensitivity suit. The difference, of course, was that if Carla faced the world unfiltered she would not have a seizure. She just didn't think she'd be able to bear it.

When she had heard the noise start up, she'd instantly known that it was an evil thing, a dangerous thing. But it hadn't touched her, because her screaming had drowned it. And as she'd walked through town, through car crashes and corpses, through Jisoo's heart-stopping collapse, the screaming had gotten louder and louder. Now she could hardly hear the sound at all anymore.

She walked through the front door of the mint-green colonial.

There was a dead man in the living room. He was white and middle-aged, wearing a Hanes T-shirt and plaid boxers. Drool crusted the stubble on his chin. Carla ignored him and went upstairs. She opened every door until she found what she wanted: a mountainous speaker set and a humming computer monitor. A white boy sat in a giant black plush desk chair, the sort of desk chair Carla could picture in a law firm or a fancy bank, with a pair of expensive headphones still dangling from his limp fingers. Carla stepped over him, moved the computer mouse to wake the screen and found some kind of music synthesizer. She clicked the pause button.

The sound disappeared. The sudden and total silence rang in Carla's ears behind the screaming.

She found the file the synthesizer was playing and moved it to the trash, which she emptied. Then she stood back and rubbed her ears. Experimentally she prodded the kid's calf with her foot. He didn't move. She kicked him again, harder. He slipped from the chair but otherwise did not react. She put her foot on his neck and applied pressure until something crunched. Nothing.

Carla, a strange heat bubbling in her throat, glanced out the window. She spotted Laila and Jisoo down the street where she'd left them, Jisoo sitting up and looking disoriented, Laila cocking her head hopefully into the silence and then fumbling for her phone. Carla did not bother to reach for her own phone. Her parents both worked on Main Street. She knew she ought to return to Jisoo and Laila, but instead she went to the boy's closet, pushed his clothes to the side, shut herself in and sat on the dusty floor. In the pitch-quiet blackness she closed her eyes and screamed.

PAGE of PENTACLES.

Willoughbuoy

~ Hermester Barrington

I suppose the phrase "imaginary friend" will work as well as any other. My uncertainty arises because he's not imaginary to *me*—but if you look over my left shoulder, close one eye and squint the other, you might be able to see him, or think that you do.

People have seen a lot of strange things when they do that—a thin tall figure with long fingers in a pale jumpsuit and bat's wings, a girl with rabbit ears in a frock, Dame Helen Mirren, my favorite actress—but most of them see a man in his thirties to fifties at a desk, leaning over a keyboard, scanning through books, scribbling notes, frowning all the while. He stands next to a window through which one can see the tops of trees—pines, most people say—on a golf course. He often supports himself with one hand on a desk—a Craftsman, I think, like my own, but not as well cared for. The light comes in as in a Vermeer painting, at an angle, and, reflected from the papers scattered on his desk, illuminating his face from beneath. Based on descriptions by those who have seen him over the years, he has aged since first he was spotted.

Mind, he's not exactly anyone I would have imagined as my imaginary friend—I would have expected some version of Prometheus, or Coyote, or that girl at the supermarket who shyly flirts with me, but we don't always get to pick our friends, do we? At least not imaginary ones.

He has only appeared directly to me once. At 3:12 AM, precisely—I don't know how I know that, because we don't have any clocks in the house—he opened the door to the bedchamber, and, frowning, stood at the end of the bed and recited that Robert Frost poem about a cord of maple logs burning slowly in the swamp. While I was figuring out how to respond, he knocked over a glass of water on the bedstand and disappeared. Getting out of bed to clean it up, I glanced out the window, and saw the lawn and the lake littered with loose pages, on which I had been writing my poetry, and which I had left on the deck . . . I went out and fetched them, the ones on the lawn I mean. When I looked up, Willoughbuoy was standing in the window, looking down at me, but he was gone by the time I got back upstairs.

I've also seen him in dreams late in the morning, when my bladder awakens me. As I debate whether I want to arise, I recall him before the memory fades—it's 5 AM, but he's already at work on his book, on ideas of progress in the Atlantic world in the 19th century, before he goes off to his day job (he's an archivist at a law firm). He mutters to himself in any number of European languages as he searches through the pages of a book, sometimes more than one at a time. He takes a sip of some soft drink, some knock off version of a much more popular heavily caffeinated citrus soda, the original being my own preferred beverage—and winces as it hits a bad tooth. I sometimes get back to sleep afterwards, but never dream of him again, if I do.

Sometimes he is writing fiction, viewers say, a novel shaped like a Klein bottle about an amateur protozoologist/haiku poet. I've heard this from people who don't know that this description fits me pretty nicely, so perhaps there's something to it.

I first learned about him some thirty years ago. My wife Fayaway and her friend, Mistress Dionaea, were discussing the best way to use magnets, a Leyden jar, and a gyroscope to figure out the exact shape of the earth, when Dionaea stopped, stared past me, and said, "Hermester, there's someone standing behind you, over your left shoulder." Our questions to Dionaea elicited the following information: he was tall and slender, with a full head of thin chestnut hair, a t shirt and jeans, and Birkenstocks. He was holding a chapbook edition of "Bartleby the Scrivener," with illustrations by Barry Moser—our copy, as it turned out, which was missing the next time I looked for it. He was standing in front of a window—the window, in fact, that I have already described. "He wants to tell you that his name is 'Willoughbuoy,'" Dionaea said then, and spelled it out and told me how to pronounce it, which brought to my mind the image of a tall slender lad bending in a breeze I could not feel. Somebody's car alarm went off then, and the vision or whatever it was disappeared.

He has borrowed or stolen a number of our books since then—usually works that would interest him, I suppose. Occasionally I find works on our bookshelves that no one remembers acquiring—*Alice in Wonderland* in the language of the Voynich manuscript; a dismembered copy of *Hopscotch* with the "chapters arranged," a handwritten note reads, "for ease of reading;" a rough draft of *The Da Vinci Code* autographed by Michael Baigent and Richard Leigh. If he is trying to tell me something by stealing my books, or leaving others, I'm not sure what it is.

I've thought about writing his book, tentatively titled *The Millennium is on the Horizon*, for him—he seems to rewrite the same chapters over and over—but maybe a book about time and fugitive progress should be impossible to finish. Someone once said that in order to be happy, you should find a project that you enjoy and which is too big to complete in your lifetime. That being said, it doesn't seem to be working for him.

I can only imagine why he might have been appearing to me over the years. Is he the dross of my realized desires? A reminder of the decades in which I lived a life of drudgery, moving through my life as if befogged? Might he be a sort of *memento mori*, or an admonition to be true to my own self? I had hoped that by writing about him, I would exorcise him, but I having drafted and revised this piece for three nights in a row, he has nonetheless appeared in my dreams on the past three mornings, and has been the focus of my mind's eye as I stumble out of bed and fumble my slippers onto my feet. As has been the case in the past, his image remained in my thoughts until I turned my hand to my pursuits—my haiku, my protozoology, my ficciones—and then, at about the same time that the dew evaporated from the leaves of the sycamores outside the windows, my memory of him faded as I turned to greet the morning sun.

ACE ᨖ CUPS.

The Mayor of Marzipan

~ Kimberly Moore

Tea & Tarot inspires fear in some people. Some condemn us. Some of them are fascinated by us. Most of them think we're full of shit, but a source of entertainment. However they may feel, the citizens of Oak Village end up in the back room with Madame Bresa eventually, full of doubt but wanting to believe so strongly that they lay an offering on her table and watch her place the mysterious cards and solve their problems. We even ushered the pastor's wife through the basement door for a reading the day after her judgmental husband fired up a mob to protest our existence. We are a forgiving business.

I'm the baker. If anyone exists in this town who has not yet allowed Bresa to read their cards, they have still eaten my work. They say my talent is wasted here, but I have no culinary degrees. I learned from my father and YouTube. I confess my lack of qualifications every time I am complimented and told I belong in a fancy hotel or a French patisserie. Years ago, before Madame Bresa arrived and invited herself to an interview with Tilly, the owner, I considered leaving for a possible pay increase. Somehow, that idea lost appeal after she arrived. Before Bresa, the fortune-tellers were only actors.

On my cutting board this morning is our mayor, George Williams, made of marzipan. Before Bresa arrived, I used store-bought, but Bresa's recipe is slightly different and she insists that I use her recipe for this ceremony. It includes honey from her bees and almonds from her source, whatever that may be. Bresa has secrets, as a tarot reader is expected, I suppose. She claims to have ancient gypsy blood, a multitude of ex-husbands, ex-wives, and ex-lovers, and now in the golden years of her life, she only wants to assist fellow humans instead of breaking hearts. I've always wanted details, but even drunk, she'll only wink and grin. "Oh, my darling Penelope, I was trouble," she'll say with her slowly enunciated words and thick Slavic accent.

Bresa appears in the kitchen just as I am admiring my Mayor Williams doll.

"Lovely," she says, looking at the photo his wife sent and then at my handiwork.

"I didn't need the photo. He's been mayor for as long as I can remember. He watched me grow up." I enjoyed adding the pigment to darken his skin, rounding his belly, forcing his belt buckle to face his feet. As plump as he has always been in my memory, he was always elegant. I fretted for hours last night with a razor designing his wrinkle-free blue suit.

"A man with a good reputation," she says as if it's extinct. Now she's frowning at the doll.

"This isn't like voodoo, is it?"

"No, no, no. You know me better than that." Bresa is petite, barely five feet tall. Her affection is always meant to be motherly, but I feel like the mother during an embrace with her head at the level of my chest. "Is he complete? His wife will be here in an hour."

I watch Bresa glide away with my masterpiece. What she does with the dolls before the client arrives is one of her many secrets. Her clients refuse to reveal the details of the ceremony, no matter how much Tilly and I have begged. "Just give us a hint," we've whispered later when we've run into them in the village. They always, without fail, happily decline.

Tilly closes the kitchen door. It must be almost time to open and I have more to do this morning than worry about my marzipan man. The Oak Village book club meets today in the main dining room, and due to Tilly's misremembering dates, the fifth birthday party for the bank president's daughter has been scheduled at the same time in the playhouse.

Tilly glances over the spread for the book club. "I thought we were going to give them more sweet than savory."

"The opposite. Remember last month when they hardly touched the sweets and ran out of savory?"

"I trust you," she chuckles. "I've been screwing up everything lately. It looks fantastic. Are we all set for the birthday party?"

"Take a look." I point her in the direction of the second kitchen island, where my purple sloth-themed cupcakes await the birthday guests.

Tilly smiles and applauds for a moment. "I love sloths!" We hear a car crunching the gravel behind the building.

"That will be Cheryl." Tilly descends to the basement to open the door for Cheryl, the mayor's wife, who request-ed a discreet arrival.

Cheryl keeps her sunglasses on when she greets me, making her appear more like an insect than usual. She and the mayor are visually incompatible. They are the same race, which is all they seem to have in common. He is short, fat, manic with the need to socialize, and imme-diately in control of every situation. Cheryl is half a foot taller than her husband and fragile in build. Her friend-liness has been rehearsed, but not perfected. Although Cheryl has never been unkind to me, I always feel she would prefer to be ignored.

"Hello, Penelope," she says without smiling. She sur-veys my work.

"Bresa's waiting for you," Tilly says, leading her to the back hallway.

Cheryl moves quickly to the door. I can't help wonder-ing what problem she might have with her husband, who at least in my eyes, has the personality of a teddy bear and leaves happy faces wherever he goes. Most customers who have asked for this ceremony have been more transpar-ent. Everyone knew the high school basketball coach was cheating on his wife, and I was asked to create his doll as a nude. I didn't ask questions, but Tilly shook her head when she saw my work, followed by a frown for his long-suffer-ing wife. The coach has spent more time at home since the ceremony. Others seemed to be fidelity-related, too, but I can't imagine that to be the problem with the mayor.

Tilly joins me in the kitchen again. "You think you know someone. How could they have problems? He's the sweetest man I've ever known. Including my dad. And yours."

"I agree. Guess we'll never know."

Once the birthday party begins, we forget the mayor. Tilly's nephews and nieces serve the book club, the auxiliary dining room, and the playhouse. There are only four of them, so Tilly and I join the chaos. Word travels between us as we burst through the kitchen door of requests and needs, mistakes, and skinned knees in the playhouse.

It is only when I see Bresa at the door to the basement that I take a moment to breathe. Bresa's expression is unfamiliar. Nothing fazes her usually, but she stares out the front windows, then turns back to the dining room, where the book club continues their debates. Seeing her uncomfortable makes me uncomfortable.

"Bresa," I whisper when the register line is empty and I can cross the room, "what's going on?"

She doesn't answer as quickly as I'd like. She looks up at me and sighs. "Cheryl changed her mind."

"So?"

"I don't know what to do with him now."

"Who?"

"The mayor!"

"George is here?"

"The mayor you made."

"Throw him away."

"You don't understand." She takes my hand and pulls me to the door of her room. "Penelope, you have to swear you'll never tell what I'm about to show you."

I shouldn't leave the register, but Bresa's message seems urgent. "I swear."

She opens the door and I see nothing at first. Then, there is motion on the floor. The wire trashcan inverted with a stack of books on top is scooting closer to me. I have to bend to see the little marzipan mayor pushing the trashcan with all the strength honey and almonds will give him.

No sleep tonight. I pretend to sleep so Mike won't stay awake and worry about me. He freaked out when I fainted at work today. He wasn't alone. I have never fainted before and it freaked me out, too. I wanted to tell him. As my husband, he needed more of an explanation than low blood sugar, which I've never suffered as a baker. I should feel worse for concocting that lie. However, the truth would have been more unbelievable.

His back is to me now, expanding and deflating with his deep sleep breath. I imagine how I would confess. I may be a criminal, although I can't imagine what the indictment would be. It's a moral dilemma I never thought I would confront—creating a type of life for the sole purpose of a ceremony. However, Bresa whispered to me while I was regaining consciousness that my creation was not a living individual.

"He's a form of thought like a memory," she said as she sprinkled a flowery liquid over my shirt and crossed my forehead with a feather. "He has no soul or will. He only knows what Cheryl communicated to him in the ceremony."

At that moment, I glanced at the moving trash can again. He seemed to have desires, and what he wanted was to get out of the trashcan. Bresa scooted him to a closet and closed the door just as Mike arrived. I found myself answering questions about pregnancy, and although I swore I wasn't, Mike insisted on a visit to my doctor.

I'm not pregnant, but that would be less troubling. I trace my finger down Mike's shoulder blade, both wanting him to wake up and not wanting to wake him. I only wake our Siamese cat who is curled behind Mike's bent knees. It's three-thirty. If I go to work now, I will have some time to observe the tiny mayor and perhaps make sense of it.

I hear the little mayor bumping into the walls of the closet while I enter the security code. How can Bresa say he's not alive? Perhaps she is minimizing his existence, the way vegetarians will kill a mosquito and rationalize it because of its size and bothersome personality. In Bresa's room, my hand shakes when I open the closet door. The trash can moves into the room and I squat to watch the miniature mayor in his continued effort to push.

To my surprise, removing the trash can does not change his activity. He pushes at air, punching and lunging forward at nothing in front of him. Bresa told me the mayor knows nothing but what Cheryl communicated to him. All he seems to know is low-effort fighting. Is this what Cheryl told him? Is he the memory of a physical fight?

He doesn't respond to my voice, nor does he see me. I observe, trying to become comfortable with my creation as he reaches a wall and pushes against it. Fifteen minutes later, I touch him. No reaction. When I lift him, he continues his pushing motions in my hands. He is as warm as when I first molded him. He appears to breathe, but I feel nothing when I place my hand in front of his tiny face, his unblinking eyes I created yesterday with a needle.

In the kitchen, I place him on the floor and watch him continue the only motion he knows, wandering under the table. I begin measuring almond flour and sugar for macarons. The routine is soothing and it seems kinder to keep him with me than to leave him in a trashcan in a dark closet. I suspect he doesn't care. If Bresa is correct, he isn't sentient. While I begin beating egg whites, I try to imagine Bresa's explanation of being a thought form or a memory. I have too many questions.

When I hear the kitchen door swing open, I expect to see Tilly or Bresa. Mike is unexpected. He stands in the doorway with his arms and mouth open, questioning me with his eyes.

"You didn't leave a note?" he asked when I turn off the mixer. "I thought you went to the ER!"

"Sorry, babe. I have lots of macarons to make today."
I've lost the mayor. I'm surveying the tiled floors when
Mike yells and stomps his foot.

"What the hell was this?" He leans on the table and lifts
his sneakered foot, attempting to shake it free of what
he has just stomped. I'm afraid to look. I recognize the
flattened blue suit.

"The mayor. You stepped on the mayor."

Bresa struggles with English sometimes, but she has no
words in any language now. Mike is no help. I scooted
a barstool into the back of his legs while I scraped the
mayor from his foot and he has sat there catatonic ever
since. He should have been at work ten minutes ago.

"Tell me what to do," I say to Bresa. She is studying the
flattened mayor, now motionless on the kitchen island
with a size twelve footprint etched into his squashed body.

"Can you redo him?" Bresa finally asks.

"I doubt it. I could make another."

"A new one won't remember."

"Does it matter?"

"I don't know. This has never happened before. I need
Cheryl to come back and finish what she started."

"Did I kill the mayor?" Mike interrupts, still focusing
on the opposite wall, his face drained of color.

"It's not voodoo," Bresa says.

I have to wave to get Mike's attention. "If you're not
going to work, I need you to call my dad and the two of

you need to finish the macarons. I'll try to reshape the mayor."

Mike takes his phone from his pocket and texts. I assume he's taking a day off. I hold the warm remains of the mayor, clear a place on my cluttered counter and begin squeezing the body into something recognizable again.

Bresa can't find Cheryl or George. Meanwhile, the ever-cackling quilting club arrives and my father and husband argue about the neatness Mike lacks patience for. "I hate this fiddly shit," he mumbles while dotting cupcakes with buttercream and applying butterflies with tweezers.

My father follows Mike, correcting his mistakes. "You're not saving us any time with your impatience."

I would reprimand both of them, but my focus must remain on the mayor. I've added nothing to what was scraped from Mike's shoe, but George the marzipan mayor seems larger than before. I put on Tilly's reading glasses to correct his face.

"The sausage rolls smell done, guys," I remind my helpers. "Cheddar puffs should go in next. You should have the sandwiches on the trays already."

"How much do quilters eat?" Mike complains as he put on oven mitts.

"They'll stay at least two hours, non-stop snacking." I'm the calm center of the storm. Tilly's nieces breeze past me with fresh, steaming teapots and orders for more, and my father and husband continue baking, decorating, and arranging. When the door swings open every few minutes, the laughter from the quilters reminds me of how much I am needed to do other things.

Tilly's eyes question me from the door.

"Bresa will have to explain," is all I can say. Many days we are overwhelmed, but Tilly treats each occurrence as the first.

The mayor begins to look like the mayor, slowly, although I can't shake the feeling that he has grown. I question why this has happened. The mayor is part of so many of my memories—all the school events he attended, smiling and cheering. He bought from all my fundraisers. I have countless certificates he signed with pride from the city of Oak Village when I competed in sports or academics. A photo of Mike and the mayor hangs in my home from the day Mike opened his landscaping business. Whatever complaint Cheryl has against him can't outweigh the good he has done. I shouldn't judge, not knowing. I know this, yet I can't stop.

I remember his replica fighting his way across the floor. Maybe he wasn't fighting. He could have been defending himself. If Cheryl attacked him, his constant pushing is logical. If he attacked Cheryl, a single punch would suffice. Once more, I tell myself not to speculate, not to judge. I wasn't there. I can't know.

Bresa returns, shaking her head. She has not found Cheryl or George. "I've left messages. I've told her it's interrogative that she comes back as soon as possible."

"Didn't you mean 'imperative'?"

Bresa sighs. "I can't believe I said that."

"She'll figure it out." She leans against my arm, the re-made body of the mayor on the cutting board in front of us. "He looks bigger. Don't you think so?"

Bresa raises her eyebrows. "You're right. Maybe the marzipan expanded?"

"Bresa, please tell me you know what you're doing."

"This has never happened before. I don't know if I can reanimate him after he was stepped on. I've never had one stay animated so long, either. We're in virgin territory, Penelope."

I follow her as she takes the mayor into her room. She locks us in and places him on her card table. I watch her at her cabinet of mysterious bottles next, measuring and mixing until she brings out a syringe full of a blue, chalky liquid.

"If this doesn't work, maybe Cheryl can still finish her part. I don't know what else to try." Bresa seems to have no expectations when she injects the liquid into the doll.

The mayor sits up, staring at Bresa for a moment while she holds her breath. His neck turns and now he focuses on me. I feel faint again, but I sit on an end table before I fall. He is different now, just sitting instead of pushing against whatever is before him. He seems conscious. I know it's not my imagination—he is larger than before.

"His memory has changed," Bresa says. "What were you thinking when you redid him?"

"I was recalling all the good things he did for our town and people in general. Why? What was the memory Cheryl gave him?"

"She wouldn't tell me. She only thought it during our ceremony and then she changed her mind when it came time to put an end to him."

"Bresa, you have to tell me what the point of this is. I'm too involved now."

She stands the mayor on his feet and watches him wobble for a moment before sitting again. "I thought I told you. He's like a memory sponge. When he is de-animated, the memory is gone forever."

"From the real mayor?"

"Yes. Only Cheryl didn't de-animate him. Your husband did, and a day late. Now he doesn't seem to remember what he remembered before. He's not pushing and fighting."

"I can't imagine him ever fighting with Cheryl like that. It wasn't his personality."

"Penelope, you can't know what people are like unless you live with them. Is Mike exactly the way you thought he would be before you married him?"

"No, but he's not violent. The surprises have been small and inconsequential."

Bresa starts to say something but she checks her phone instead. "It's Cheryl, finally. She's sorry. She's at her brother's house but she can come first thing tomorrow morning."

I'm relieved, although after reviewing everything Bresa has told me, I'm not sure I should be. "Maybe no damage has been done at all. Right? Nobody knows anything."

She shrugs and pulls a cardboard box from the closet. The mayor is still content to sit and do nothing. He doesn't fight when Bresa places him in the box, interlocks the flaps, and puts the box in the closet. "We'll find out tomorrow. I'd feel better if I knew where the real mayor was and what he remembered."

In bed, Mike analyzes his involvement in an attempt to absolve himself from murder charges. It's simple enough. I remind him numerous times that the mayor was not a voodoo doll, and all Mike had done was step on a cookie. Furthermore, we have no reason to believe the mayor is dead.

The thought of the marzipan mayor trapped in a box all night tortures me. Mike reminds me the doll doesn't need to breathe, or use a toilet, or eat or drink. If Bresa is right, it isn't alive at all, and its ability to move is only a reflex.

"Tomorrow, it will all be over, one way or another," Mike says as he picks up his phone. "It's late. We should sleep."

I kiss him again.

"One more thing. Promise me you'll never make a version of me in marzipan."

It was unlike Tilly to leave a door unlocked. "Hello?" I announce, leaning in. The interior looks normal, maybe slightly untidy by Tilly's standards. Yesterday was a busy day, though. Sometimes there are mistakes and in this small town, locks are rarely necessary. No one answers, and no other cars are here. I proceed to the safe, which is undisturbed. The register contains some cash, satisfying me that the open door means nothing.

Bresa's door is also open. Whoever cleaned last night must have forgotten that Bresa's cash drawer is separate. Turning into Bresa's room, my eyes are drawn to the open closet. The cardboard box appears to have burst open, torn, and unfolded on the floor.

I knew leaving him in a box was wrong.

I search now, corners and under tables, every dining room. I don't want to believe the obvious. The marzipan mayor has wandered away somewhere. My creation, easily traced to this business and me, is loose in Oak Village. Bresa and I will have to move.

"Penelope?" It's Cheryl, still wearing sunglasses, leaning in the open front door. "I am supposed to see Bresa?"

"Come in. She's not here yet, but you can wait in her room."

She moves slowly. I doubt she has slept, like the rest of us who are involved. "Did you lose something?"

I stop searching. "It's gone, I guess. I'll be in the kitchen."

I don't know who to call. Instead, I stand for a moment at the refrigerators, picturing the little mayor being run over by a truck and also realizing I need to make puff pastry. The thoughts are incompatible. I feel paralyzed.

The knock at the back door startles me.

"Penelope? Is that you?" It's the real mayor, George Williams, his face against the small window in the door. "I'm looking for Cheryl!"

At least the mayor is alive. Mike will be relieved, as will Bresa. I unlock the door. "Forgive my slow reaction, Mr. Williams. I haven't been sleeping well."

"Is everything alright? How is Mike?"

"No problems, really." It's good to see his smiling face. Like the rest of us, though, he seems tired. I've never seen him in a jogging suit, either. He seems a little lopsided. "Cheryl is in Bresa's room."

"Good to see you, Penelope."

Seeing the real mayor has alerted me to reality, at least. I gather blocks of butter for the pastry and take the rolling pin from the island cabinet.

Cheryl screams before I can begin pounding the butter. Peeking into the dining room, I see them—Cheryl walking backward, her face petrified in terror. "But you're dead!" she screeches.

He reaches forward and pushes her several times, making her stumble toward the door to the basement. One final push and she falls back through the door, thumping and thudding to the basement. What I'm thinking can't be—just because the mayor was pushing her the way the marzipan mayor was—it has to be a coincidence. What had she meant when she said he was dead?

I hear nothing. Again, I peek into the dining room.

The mayor turns his head in my direction, then his uneven body. It's his familiar grin, but when his lips part, honey streams from the corners of his mouth.

Del Mar

~ Katherine L. P. King

You emerge from the sea with a gasp: your first in the vast expanse of space above the water. Salt stings your nose, and the light stings your eyes. It's white, not yellow as you imagined when you were still beneath the surface of the waves. The blue sky looks impossibly large and empty. You kick and splash and splutter your way to shore, where you lie in the soft dry sand. It clings to your brown skin. There are tiny hairs all over you where there never were before. You laugh; it is the first time you have heard your own voice. You lie eagle-spread, staring up into the blue.

You teach yourself to stand, and then to walk. You are thoroughly unprepared for how hard it is to move, how the air around you resists your movements rather than propels them. Your body is heavy. Your manhood swings freely and your feet are a marvel. You look back at the water and imagine them there, wishing you luck. Eventually you leave the sand and begin to walk on the hot dirt of the road, heading into the bright city in the valley below.

As instructed, you go to Morado. Morado is old, skinny, twenty years on land, and quiet. He gives you what was promised: papers, clothing, some local currency, and a slip of paper on which is a handwritten address. Still stumbling occasionally, you don the clothes and follow Morado's garbled instructions to the address. As you go, the colors, smells, and sounds of the city assault you. You realize you have been living with a blanket over these senses and though you are anxious and sweating, which is entirely new, you pause to smell meat frying at a street cart, or to listen to a woman leaning out a window and strumming a small wooden instrument you cannot name.

Morado's directions lead you to a red building, low, smelling of some strong spice. You knock at the door. There is no response. You knock again, louder, the wood splintering into your fist, and someone shouts before the door flies open and a tiny old woman lets you in. She leads you to a hot kitchen where several pots boil on the stove and men sit on over-turned buckets or crates, some peeling potatoes, others slicing onions, still others splitting open and removing seeds from chilies, their eyes red and their noses running.

The woman makes you sit on the last empty crate, hands you a dirty potato and a dull knife, and scurries away. You do not look at the other men, who are all looking at you. Instead you watch to see where your peeled potatoes should go—into a large pot of salted water on the table. You have never eaten potatoes before. When you feel their eyes are no longer on you, you examine the other men in turn. Their skins have been cracked and dried by the sun, like the flesh of dead clams. Their eyes are far away; most are brown, some are blue. Some men shake with exhaustion. One, a friendlier looking youth, turns to you.

¿Cómo te llamas?

You have prepared for this question, but the word still sticks in your throat.

T-trullo.

¿De dónde?

You stare. He speaks so fast. You are not even sure he asked a question. His eyes are crystalline. When you don't answer, he nods.

¿Del mar?

You hesitate again; the young man holds his hand parallel to the floor and lets it rise and fall in a rolling motion. His hand is like the waves, swelling and crashing. Suddenly, you want only to be back there, under the surf, in the blue. You blink away tears and nod. The man points to the others in the group with blue eyes and repeats: *Del mar. Del mar. Y yo, del mar.*

The next morning, you wake before the sun. You follow the others, keeping your head down, wanting to give no indication that you dreamed of home all night.

You all climb into the back of a roaring old truck and ride away from the rising sun. The tiny old woman hands out food—hot beans in a warm corn tortilla. You eat slowly. The warmth is so unexpected and so welcome.

When the truck stops, you are in a large green field. Each of you takes a wooden bucket and you walk into the field, stoop, and begin picking. When your bucket is full of shiny red peppers you trade it for an empty one. When the sun is hot and sweat drips down your back you are allowed to sit in the minimal shade of the truck, sipping lukewarm water and eating rice and beans. You listen to the others and try to learn their language. You begin to recognize some words: *papas. Arroz con habichuelas. Concha. Trabajo.* Soon you are back in the fields.

On the ride back, the truck scales a mountain and you can see, for only a moment, a strip of blue that is the sea.

At the end of the day, a large man with thick hair on his chest hands out paper to each of you. You stuff it in your shoe and sleep with the shoes next to your pillow. It is nowhere near enough.

On the rare evening when there is no kitchen work to do, you go out. The sky darkens to black impregnated with bright stars in a spray, like sea foam. The cobblestone streets are warm from baking in the sun all afternoon, and lanterns and candles cast pools of flickering light down the winding roads. Huge crowds mill around buildings, hanging out of windows, stumbling in the streets reeking of tequila. You join a crowd around a hot grill that smells like cumin and animal fat and when you push your way to the front and finally capture the attention of the cook, you order a tripleta. Soon enough he hands you a huge greasy sandwich which you devour as you walk. As you reach the last bit of bread and pork someone bumps your arm, hard, and you drop it. Turning, you catch a fist with the side of your face and lash out, but miss. When your vision clears you see a drunken man reeling in front of you with fists raised, his eyes rolling and unfocused. You turn away and hear him curse you, spit at you. *Sirena.*

It is six months before you can leave the little red house. You get a new job washing dishes at a restaurant. It is much better money and though the work is still grueling, at least you are not drying in the sun like a stranded starfish. Your apartment is hot, empty but for the cockroaches, and a long walk from work, but you are grateful, especially since now that it is winter, there are fewer fields to be picked. You work late every night. In the day you walk the streets, smelling the sea mist, singing along to songs, and sampling food. Your favorite is tostones, with rice and beans. The hot crunch and garlic aftertaste send a thrill down your spine.

You make your way to the sea at least once a week. It is so big and bright. You cannot remember exactly what it was like there. But you miss it—and them.

You send all the money you can. Sometimes your boss at the restaurant lets you work doubles and you send it all save enough to pay your rent and feed you.

After a year, you've sent enough to bring your oldest son. You meet him at the shore on a cool, crisp morning. His body is now brown and hairy like yours. You greet him with a soft towel, welcoming him as you were not. His hair is now a curly mop of black. He smells of salt and gets white sand all over him as he stumbles around, trying to get used to his feet, already learning to live without the embracing swell of the sea.

You show him all you have learned and seen so far: *café con leche,* the colorful streets, the clubs at night. He is amazed but he misses home. He gets a job as a server in the restaurant where you wash dishes, since he picks up the language faster. He makes lots of tips, being a beautiful boy, and sends it all home. You cannot convince him to save some for himself or to come out with you and drink away the exhaustion and the homesick.

It is on a night like this you meet Ascención. Ascención is twelve years your junior, small but supple, dark haired, dark skinned, quiet but confident. It is not long before she comes to your place, her heels clunking up the stairs, her compact body hidden by a sparkling black dress.

Your son ignores you both. You do not speak to him as you and Ascención leave the kitchen, chilled beers in hand, and close your bedroom door behind you. The beers are abandoned as you fight each other out of your clothes. Then she is there, and hot, wet, sweet. You've never known it like this, these warm flushes of pleasure circling through you.

Later, Ascención falls asleep in your twin bed so you go check on your son. He is curled up so tight on his mattress in the front room of your apartment. The only thing you can see is his face, constricted even in sleep.

He looks like his mother. You try not to think of her while you are with Ascención.

Ascención likes dates: seaside restaurants, overnight stays in nearby hotels, trips up the coast. You have to send less money back or you will not be able to make rent. Your son notices and you shout at him. Your hard earned money sent away, and it is still not enough?

Ascención will not move in with you. She has a place, she says. You wonder if you are the only one she is seeing. Still, she spends most nights at your apartment, which you furnish to her liking: a stereo system, a large television with all the channels, cabinets full of food and a bathroom full of soaps, towels, cleaning supplies. You search for a two-bedroom so your son can have his own room. You get a second job bagging groceries at a small store nearby, and ask for more nights off from your dish-washing job so you can take Ascensción out. The money is never enough. You send home less and less.

One day, Ascensción comes to you at the grocery store on your break. Her dark eyes are red around the edges. *¿Que pasa?* you ask, taking her cool hands in your own, blistered from work.

Estoy embarazada. Pregnant.

You stare. Then you grin. You hug her tight to you and shout scrambled words of joy in two languages. When you release her, she smiles and kisses you. The rest of your shift flies by in a brightly-colored whirl of faces and lights.

You walk home along white cobblestones. The sun sets on the ocean, glints of light catching your eye. A part of you wonders how it ever meant more to you than scenery.

When you reach the top of the stairs and open the door to your apartment, your son is there, with a bag. He is leaving.

Hijo, no. Por favor.

He does not speak to you in that language, and pretends not to hear. Forget about me, he says, grabbing his bag and pushing past you. Forget about us.

Ascención is in the hallway, a hand pressed to her throat.

You watch your son descend the stairs, sling his bag over his shoulder, and walk off into the darkening streets.

Later that month, you have a choice to make. There are sixty-eight dollars left over from your last paycheck, after the bills, and the money you spent on Ascención, and your food. You can send it home. But why? You think of Ascención, here and now, a little baby—your baby—growing inside her. Silently, you tuck the money away.

You and Ascención do not go out so much anymore, since she cannot drink. You drink at home instead, and miss the days when you could go out alone, eating mofongo on the street, engulfed in the clear, bright light, smelling the salt water. One evening you do go out and stay drunk until the sun begins to rise. You walk around the island until you find the shore. You climb the rocks and explore the tide pools. You find the creatures which were once your neighbors. You poke at them with stubby fingers. Then you sit with your feet in the water and cry. You cannot go back.

When you get home, Ascención sits at the table with her head down. You enter and she gets up.

Me voy. Voy a hacerme un aborto.

You do not answer her. You do not breathe as she walks around you, gathers a bag, and shuts the door behind her. You do not move as the apartment settles in its emptiness.

Suddenly you have more money than you can spend, but you do not send it. You are no longer sure if they would take it. You quit your job at the restaurant and soon become a cashier at the grocery store. You spend as much time out, with friends or women, as you can. The thought of the sea burns enough that you stop thinking of it, and those you left behind, entirely, for years.

One sunny morning, you follow the sound of a crowd to a street full of tents, some kind of arts fair. You shuffle down the aisle of starched white tents where hopeful, wide-eyed creators peddle their wares: beaded bracelets, crucifixes on long silver chains, homemade soaps and bars of lotion, leather pouches and belts, small knives, braided ropes and flowers arranged in glass vases. The colors are so bright, the shapes so clean and clear.

One tent has paintings hung up on the exterior walls. You see one that gives a view of the sky from under deep, deep water. It is the kind of perspective only one of your kind could possibly know; it is far too detailed to have been imagined. The sun in the painting is a shimmery blur, obscured by the layers of aquamarine and turquoise and azure. You stare at the picture for so long that your body is stiff when you finally move. You circle the tent to look at each painting, all as beautiful as the first, each unique. Some have faces in them—faces you recognize.

When you come to the front, you see a teenage boy sitting at a card table. He looks at you, bored. Your voice is
thick when you speak.

   ¿Este tu arte?

The boy, his expression unchanged, taps a little paper
sign taped to the front of the table he sits at. On the paper
is a woman's name. You know it better than you know
your own, though it has been years since you've spoken
it.

   ¿Dónde está?

She's not here, the boy says. *No está aquí. En su galería
de arte.*

You look deep into his eyes. They are your own, not
only because you have come from the same place. He
stares back.

Do I know you? *¿Quién eres?*

You shake your head. *No. Soy un extraño para ti.* You
walk away with the words pulsing in your ears like waves:
I am a stranger.

PAGE of WANDS.

These Waters

~ M. Shedric Simpson

The hands that drew me up were not the hands that had pushed me down.

"It's okay," she said. Her eyes were brown, and her skin was dark, and her fingers wrapped tight around my wrists. "I've got you." She pulled, and I fell onto the rocky shore beside her.

A dull and listless light accosted me, and I squeezed my eyes shut. Anything seemed searingly bright after those silt-clouded depths.

"I'm Asha," the girl said. "Can you talk?"

I drew a breath and forced out the word. "Yes," I said, surprised to find it was true. I still felt the memory of water flooding my lungs, like a clenched fist inside my breast. "I think so." I looked up and she smiled at me.

It was a warm smile, but sad too. It was the smile I'd seen on my mother's face when she was reminiscing. "Do you remember how you got here?"

A beer bottle skating across the ground. The bright stab of pain on the back of my skull. The world spun before I even understood it was the bottle that had struck me. "I was walking by the river," I said. "But something happened."

Hey! Fucker! The words rang in my head. The pickup truck skidded to a halt, and four boys piled out of the bed in the back. A boot crashed into my ribs, and my body curled up like a pillbug's. *Go back to where you came from!*

"It's okay if you don't remember," Asha said. She tucked a twist of unruly brown hair behind her ear. "A lot of people don't."

But I remembered it too well. The flurry of words and blows that rained down. *Shit, look at him bleed!* the boy said, but I couldn't see it, all I could see was the muddy brown sky. *I ain't going to jail for no chink. You better finish what you started.*

I felt my hands twisting, and I looked away from Asha, not wanting her to see what was written on my face. Humiliation, rage, and hate formed a knot inside my heart; their threads cut through me like burning steel. "I drowned," I told her.

"We all did."

I tried to struggle when they dragged me into the river. I was still fighting when the blonde boy pushed my head beneath the water. But I was too weak. I'd always been smaller than the other boys. Whorls of silt blotted out the sky, and I couldn't hold my breath any longer.

"All?" I glanced around. We weren't alone on the shore. Other figures huddled beneath the murky sky. Children, all of them. A few were barely more than infants.

"About a hundred of us, now. There weren't so many when I came here." She placed her hand over mine. "If you're ready, I'll show you around."

"I'd like that," I said. Anything was better than reliving those moments over and over again. I pulled off my right shoe and placed it on the rock. I'd lost the other in the river, and I didn't think I'd see it again.

I shoved my socks into my pockets as Asha led me away from the shore. The soil was warm beneath my bare feet, as if heated by the sun, though I couldn't tell if it was night or day. A persistent breeze swept in from the water, cold and metallic and tasting of stone.

"Let's go up the hill," she said. "There's a fire, and you can get a view of the whole island."

I looked beyond her shoulder at the landscape above. Figures nestled amidst the pale grass that covered the slope. Some slept, curled into tight balls, while others stared out across the water in some long and silent vigil. Few seemed to notice our passage.

The grass was waist-deep and silken to the touch. I found myself yearning to lie down in it as well, but I followed Asha up the well-worn footpath instead. We passed a dwarf tree, leafless and skeletal. Dark bulbous fruit hung from its branches.

Asha grasped one. The tree shivered in protest, but relented. She pressed the fruit into my hand. "You can eat these," she said. "Actually, there isn't much else to eat. I tried catching fish once, but they smelled wrong."

"Wrong?"

She shrugged. "Like they'd died days ago, even though they were still moving. So I just let them go."

I nodded and held onto the fruit as she turned back to

the trail. It felt warm in my hand. "What's wrong with the children? Why aren't they playing, or doing anything?"

"They're waiting," she said. "Some leave as soon as they get here, but for others . . . It's been a long time."

"How long have you been here?"

She glanced down at her feet. I couldn't see the look on her face, but her voice was ragged when she answered. "I don't really know anymore."

I didn't push her any further. We turned at the switch-back and headed up along the ridge. The view opened up around us. The island was made of three low hills, all dressed in the same pale fields, and fringed with jagged black rocks. Across the water to my left and right lay the distant banks of the great river, though I could see nothing of what waited there. Faint points of light drifted across the span between them, crossing always toward my left, against the course of the wind.

The trail cut away from the ridge and into a small hollow near the top of the hill. A group of children huddled around a campfire there. Asha caught my hand and drew me towards them. A boy in a faded tank top stared at me with bright blue eyes. His skin was white and his hair was the color of dust.

"You're new," he said.

"My name's Lee." My father had spelled my name with the hanzi, but I always pictured it the way my mother had written it.

"I'm Toby," he said. He looked up at Asha. "One of them is leaving."

"Where?"

He stood and pointed down the slope. "Over there. He just started walking. Should we do anything?"

"It's his time," Asha said. "He has to go."

She let go of my hand and moved beside Toby. I stepped next to her and gazed down the hill until I saw it too. A boy walking through the waxen field below. He might have been twelve at most; the grass came up halfway up his chest. None of the other children moved to stop him as he walked toward the shore.

"Where is he going?"

"Out there," Asha said. "One of those boats."

When she said it, I could see them for what they were. The tiny drifting lights were lanterns, hung from the prows of boats that crossed between the two banks. A lone figure sat in each. "They're crossing over," I said. "The souls of the dead."

"I think so."

It didn't surprise me the way I thought it should have. I had died. It stood to reason that the others here had died as well. Some part of me had known it ever since I'd climbed back out of the water. "What about the boy?"

"Watch."

The boy pulled off his shirt as he reached the shoreline, then waded waist-deep into the water. He dropped the shirt, and the current pulled it downstream. His shoulders trembled, and then he dove. The river devoured him with barely a ripple. A few seconds later it was as if he'd never existed.

"I see him," Toby said.

I strained against the uneasy light. A flicker of movement pierced the surface—an iridescent shimmer where there should have been a boy. It slid further out into the depths. A jagged fin. The serpentine twist of a coiling tail. Out, and deeper, until I could no longer track it.

We stood in silence for a long minute. The wind that wrapped around the island sent waves through the fields beneath us and painted whitecaps on the water. Toby sucked in a deep breath, and I felt myself do the same, tensing in anticipation.

One of the drifting lights flickered out. The silhouette of the boat vanished.

"He made it," Toby said. His voice was sad.

"Of course he did," Asha answered. "You will too, one day. I promise."

"Mmhmm."

Asha turned back to the fire, and I did too. We sat down on rocks. The other three children never glanced up, only stared into the flames with the ruminative gaze of ancient pyromancers.

"What happened out there?" I asked. "What was that boat?"

"He found the person who'd drowned him," Asha said. "And carried them to the depths, so now they'll never cross over. He'll feast on their flesh for eternity."

My chest tightened. "Is that all we're here for? Just waiting—just waiting for that?"

"To set things right. To punish the ones who murdered us," she said. "That's what we're waiting for."

I still held the fruit in my hands, and I tore it open to focus on something else. The flesh inside was white, and filled with pockets of glistening black seeds. Like a pomegranate in monochrome. I slid one of the seeds past my lips and held it between my tongue and the roof of my mouth until it disintegrated. It was sweet, almost too sweet at first, but it drew my mind away from the taut wires inside my breast.

"Can I get some wood for the fire?" I asked Asha at last.

"It just burns," she said. "It always has. I think it's not really a fire. Just—the memory of a fire."

I nodded, though I didn't understand. I itched for something to do. I was like my father in that way. His hands had never been idle. I still remembered the grass stains on his fingers when he'd grabbed me and lifted me up to the sky.

My father had come with the factory, but when the factory moved away, he'd stayed for me and my mother. There were no jobs for a foreign engineer in town, so he took what work he could find. He trimmed hedges and fixed motors. He made sure there was always food on the table and new shirts in my closet. If there was ever any despair inside his heart, he channeled it into his work and never let it show. Not even on the day he died. I still remember Mrs. Siegel shouting at him from her porch when he collapsed in the middle of her yard. He kept trying to stand up and push the mower, even after his heart had stopped.

I swallowed another pomegranate seed and looked at Asha. "So there's nothing to do? No work?"

Her eyes burned. "This is our work. Keeping watch. Waiting for our time."

"Who are you waiting for, then?"

Her mouth twisted. "I don't know. I don't remember much of what came before this. Just glimpses here and there. Flames and darkness. Water, like ice inside my lungs. Someone calling my name."

I shook my head. "If you don't know who you're waiting for, how will you know when they cross?"

"Everyone knows. They always do," she said. "Whoever did this—" She pulled the collar of her dress to the side, and I saw the puckered scar beneath her clavicle. "I'll know when they come."

I knew I was asking the wrong questions, but it was too late to stop. "If you don't even know who it was, then why not let it go? Just walk away?"

"Don't you think people have tried? We can't just leave." She glared at me. "There's a reason that we're here."

I opened my mouth to protest, but she stood up and turned away. "I'm going for a walk."

"I'm sorry," I called after her, but she didn't respond. There was only the faint rustling as her figure parted the pale grasses, and then the cold wind stole even that.

"It's okay," Toby said. "She'll be back."

The flames whirled. I held out my hands and caught a whisper of warmth, or maybe it was only the memory of warmth.

"I think she's been here a long time," he said. "I think it's hard for her to keep waiting."

He didn't look more than six, but I wondered how long he'd lingered here. "I shouldn't have pushed her."

Toby wrapped his arms around his knees and shivered. "It's not really you that she's mad at. It's me."

"Why would she be mad at you?"

He frowned. "Because I'm leaving soon, and she'll still be here."

I saw the way his legs shook, just like the shoulders of the boy who'd walked into the river. I saw his eyes, wide and darting. "You can feel it," I said.

"But I don't want to."

"It's nothing to be scared of. Asha said it's what we're here for."

"But she didn't mean to do it. I know she didn't. She was just upset."

"What do you mean?"

"My mom. She would have come back for me, if the car hadn't fallen in the river. I know she would have." He looked up at me with eyes that shone desperately. "I don't want to hurt her."

"Then don't," I said. "Don't go." I felt sick to my stomach.

"But you said it too. It's why we're here. We have to go."

"I was wrong. Go somewhere else. Anywhere but here."

He shook his head. "I can feel it pulling me already."

"I'm sorry." The words weren't enough, but they were all I had.

"It's okay," he said. "It's just what happens, right? Maybe I don't have to hurt her. Maybe I can just hold her, like I used to before the river." He turned his eyes back to the flames. "She was always nice to me, even when she was sad."

My hands curled into fists and my thoughts twisted against each other. I didn't know who I hated more. The mother who'd drowned him in the river, or the world that had cast him up on these shores just to torture her. I saw the face of the blonde boy, shoving me beneath the water. The ripples distorted his face. My jaw ached from clenching, or maybe it was just the memory of pain. I forced myself to eat another pomegranate seed, chewing it mechanically. "I'm sure she loved you," I said.

The flames were silent, without any of the crackle and roar of the school bonfire last month. The quiet made the sky above us feel enormous and heavy. I leaned closer to the fire, watching the embers spiral skyward. I don't know if I dreamt, or even if I slept, but I know that time passed in that timeless place, and it was only Toby's restless stirring that brought me back to myself.

His face was taut with worry. I wished I could believe the story he'd told himself, but I knew Asha was right. All of us here had been murdered. There was a reason we were here. "Can't sleep?" I asked.

"No," he answered. "You?"

I shook my head.

"The fruit helps sometimes. Make it easier to rest." He glanced over his shoulder at the river. "But Asha won't eat it anymore."

"I don't think I need it either." I understood her anger; I was wrong to have denied it to her. I wanted to let mine burn, but I hated the feeling that I was being used by this place.

"I wanted to wait until she came back," Toby said. He hugged his legs against his chest. "Will you come with me instead?"

"Is it time?"

His breaths were quick and shallow. He nodded.

I stood and took his hand. He climbed shakily to his feet. "I'm scared."

"Everything's going to be okay," I said. My mother had told me the same thing, with sad dark eyes, before my father's funeral. But when we'd gotten home, she'd held me when I cried for hours.

We followed the winding path through the fields of pale grass, until we came to the river's edge. Toby stepped onto the bare rock and looked up at me. "I don't want to go."

I knelt, so that we were eye to eye. "Then stay," I told him.

He shivered and pulled away from me, but I caught his other hand and held him. He craned his head to look over his shoulder. "It won't let me." Panic tugged at his voice. "Help me. Please."

I pulled him close and wrapped my arms around him. "Of course." I didn't have any choice. My mother would have done the same in a heartbeat.

Every muscle in his body pulled taut, and he froze like a panicked deer, until his body erupted in tremors. His flesh turned to ice, so cold that it burned my arms. He uttered a choked sob. "Don't let me go. Please. Don't let go."

"I won't," I said. "I promise."

I kept hold of him, but the trembling didn't pass. He cried out, and his skin peeled away. Glittering scales rippled along his shoulder. Bones twisted unnaturally beneath his tank top. I clutched him against my chest, desperate to stop the change. Spined fins erupted from his shoulder blades. I gasped as they tore through my arms, but I didn't let go. There were no fins. I felt no pain. It was just the memory of pain.

There were no words to his cries, just a plaintive whimper that went on and on. The uneasy sky whirled overhead. The pale shoulder beneath my cheek was sometimes skin, sometimes scales, and sometimes both at once. His tears soaked the back of my shirt.

I pulled him against me, rocking gently. His breath came in ragged gulps. Slits flared along his neck, then sealed shut again. My mother would have sung to him, but I had my father's voice, so I just held him until the shaking stopped.

The scales crumbled into shimmering dust, and the wind carried them away. The boy sucked in a lungful of air, then let it out slowly. "She's gone," he said. "She's gone."

I released him, and he took a timid step back. "She's gonna be okay," I said. "You are too."

Toby slipped his hand inside mine as I stood back up, and we stood and watched the boats crossing in silence. I knew that one of them would call to me, one day. My flesh would writhe, and I would go out to meet the boy that had pressed me under the water. But I remembered my father too, lifting me up as if he were returning a constellation to the sky.

"You shouldn't have done that." Asha's voice rang out behind me.

I realized that my hand was empty. I turned, but there was no sign of Toby. I hoped that wherever he'd gone was somewhere better than what this place had meant for him. "It was what he wanted," I said.

Asha stood at the edge of the field, her mouth drawn into an angry slash. There were other children too. Some looked on with horror, others wide-eyed with wonder.

She shook her head. "That wasn't right."

I took a deep breath. I held the air inside of me, dark and metallic and tasting of stone. "Maybe that's for each of us to decide." I peeled off my shirt and dropped it on the black rocks. The cold wind wrapped around my body. "Maybe there's a reason we're here, but I have to believe that there's something more." I turned away, feeling Asha's accusing eyes upon me. "I don't know what's waiting over there, but I'm going to find out."

I waded out into the river. Gravel shifted beneath my feet, and I fought for balance. Waves crashed around my waist, pushing me toward the shore. For every step I took, the river only cast me further back. There was a weight inside of me—a knot that hung like an anchor from my heart. The image of the boy who'd held me under. Like a sickly jewel, it gleamed in my mind. Full of hate and heavier than anything. But I didn't need it anymore. It belonged to this place, and I did not. I cut the threads that bound it one at a time, all the shame and hurt and bitterness, until the current carried it away.

I felt my father's hands lifting me up. My mother's hands wrapped around me. Those were the hands that mattered. Boats drifted like fireflies in the distance, drawn always toward that distant shore. Like the promise of daybreak, I would reach it too.

The water embraced me, and I swam.

Dinner Time

~ Erica Sage

Every day was dinner for Janice Godspeed.

Every damn day.

"John," she called.

"Mary," she called.

And the children raced to the table, insatiable.

The plates lay ready at their places. Her husband, fork poised in the air, waited at his seat.

The children grabbed their forks, hands in fists, prongs to the ceiling. All eyes were on Janice, heads tipped back and ready. Their eyes big and ready. Lips moist and ready. Tip of the tongue, ready.

Janice went to the garage for the tool box. She carried it to the dining room and set it on the floor next to the table.

"How was school today?" she asked as she lay her napkin across her lap.

"Stupid," John said.

"Boring," Mary said.

The children leaned toward their mother, eager for dinner.

"And how was work?" Janice asked her husband Gary.

"Marty said he'll stop by," he answered instead. Janice's brother always stopped by for dinner.

Janice leaned down to the toolbox next to her chair, unclicked the hinged, and took out the heavy sheers. She held her hair taut with her left hand, and positioned the sheers against her scalp with her right hand. The blades cut through in one effort. She placed the chunk of hair on John's plate. His fork dove in, lifted the strands, and he spun the strands around the prongs. He didn't wait for his sister before he took it into his mouth. Janice did the same with the hair on the right side of her head. This went to Mary. The hair at the back, which she held taut above her head in order to reach it with the sheers, went to her husband.

Dinner was a bit later tonight. Her family was famished. They shoved strands into their mouths.

"You need to chew your food," Janice said.

The children looked up.

"Oh, gawd," they said, disgusted.

This got her husband's attention. "Jan, baby. It makes it really hard to eat when we've got to look at you."

She'd heard this before. She set the sheers on the table, went to the closet, and grabbed a scarf to put over her nearly bald scalp.

Scarf tied under her chin, she picked up the sheers. She used them to cut her fingernails, and she put the nails in three teacups. She added her toenails too. She gave them each a cup.

"That's not so bad," her husband said, looking at the nails, not her hands.

The doorbell rang.

The door opened before she had a chance to stand.

Marty. He nodded brusquely and shut the door behind him. He dragged a chair from the kitchen, took a place between the children.

"Uncle Marty!" they cheered.

Janice sighed. She leaned over the tool box, replacing the sheers. She took out a butcher knife.

She leaned back in her chair and placed her foot in front of her brother. He was too busy sneaking her nails out of the children's teacups to notice.

"Can you help at least?" Janice said.

Marty took the knife. "Can you hold still at least?"

"I haven't moved an inch."

Marty lifted his arm up above his head and came down hard. Her foot rolled on its side and fell off the table.

"Gawd, mom," the children said.

"Do you have to do that at the table?" her husband asked, mouth open in disgust, a fingernail stuck in the gap between his front teeth.

"There isn't any silverware," Marty said.

Janice stood. She hopped on her one foot toward the kitchen, lost her balance, grabbed hold of the wall. She hopped again, rested on the back of a couch. Hopped again toward the silverware drawer, caught herself on the counter.

"Mom!" John called.

"Mom!" Mary called.

Of course they were still hungry. Janice knew that hair and nails would never be enough. "One moment, please."

The telephone rang.

Janice hopped toward the phone, silverware in hand.

The phone rang again.

Janice hopped.

"Jeezus Christ," her husband said. "I'll get it." He shoved his chair back, stood, and snatched the phone off the receiver. "Hello?" he barked. "Oh. Hey, Sherry," said Gary, ever so sweet.

Janice, finally returned to the table, handed the silverware and napkin to her brother.

Her husband continued, "Yeah. Always. Of course." He placed the phone on the receiver. "Your mom is on her way."

"Grandma!" The children cheered.

"You better get something on the table before she gets here," Marty said, as he used his steak knife to cut off the big toe.

"Is my father coming?" Janice asked Gary.

"She didn't mention it, but you know he always shows up sooner or later."

That was true.

Janice stood and made her ungainly way back to the kitchen for more silverware and plates.

"Kids, help your mom," Gary said.

But no one moved. They nibbled at the nails and watched Uncle Marty cut each toe off and pop them into his mouth. Janice brought the silverware in one trip, the plates in a second.

"Can you just give me one piece, Uncle Marty?" John asked. "You never share."

That was also true. So, by the time Janice fell back into her seat at the table, the kids were glaring at her.

She kept the butcher knife on the table. She'd need it later, and probably Marty would too when he had eaten all the toes.

Janice took out the bone saw. She lifted her dress to her hips and tucked it under her rump. She positioned the saw at a diagonal below her pubic bone. She started sawing. The blade dragged across the skin, pulled at the tendons. The bone was unyielding. She adjusted her angle. She was sweating with the effort. Perhaps the blade wasn't sharp enough.

Her husband coughed. "You're gonna need the electric saw," he said, not looking at her, but at one of her hairs he'd pulled out of his throat.

She placed her one foot on the floor, away from the blood that would no doubt send her slipping to the floor, and braced herself against the table. Once up, she hopped back to the kitchen, using the same route as before. Her leg, not fully attached now, swung awkwardly with each bounce. Finally in the garage, she found the electric saw. She was slow returning to the table. Though, with mouths full for the moment, her family hadn't seemed to notice her absence.

Janice plugged the saw into the outlet nearest her chair. She clicked the switch, and it roared to life. The kids started and plugged their ears.

"Do you have to be so loud?" they shouted at her.

Janice put the saw in the wound, pressed it against the bone. It shifted and bounced. "I think the blade is pinched," she said. The family shook their heads at her. "I think it's pinched!" she shouted.

Her husband shrugged and leaned back, picking at his teeth. With her left hand, she pushed on her knee to bend back the bone, to give the blade some room to cut through. Her leg, finally loose, lobbed to its side and hit the floor with a thud.

A spatter of blood hit her daughter's shoe. Indignant, Mary gaped at her mother. Her brother handed her a napkin.

Janice bent down and picked up the leg, set it on the table. She stood, leaned against the table with her right hip, and positioned the saw just above the knee. As the saw whirred, she pushed until the leg fell in two large parts. She lay the thigh on her son's plate, her calf on her daughter's.

"I don't want the part by her butt," John said.

"I don't want the part by her foot," Mary said.

The doorbell rang, and the door opened. Her mother came in. "You didn't bother to wait?" she said to her daughter.

"I'll get you a chair, Ma," Marty offered, his mouth full of meat, Janice's heal in his hand.

"I'd appreciate that," she said, glaring at Janice.

Janice picked up the butcher knife. She placed her left hand, palm flat on the table where her plate should be. She chopped off her left hand, and set it on Mary's plate. She moved her calf to her mother.

"I'll share this with your father when he gets here," her mother said, reaching for a knife and fork.

The doorbell rang again.

Gary looked to Janice.

Janice shrugged. She simply couldn't get up at this point.

Gary resigned to opening the door himself. But it wasn't Janice's father, as expected. It was their neighbor, Mrs. Greely, who lost her husband the year before to cancer.

"I don't mean to be a bother, but I saw you were hosting others, so I just thought I'd stop by for a family meal."

Janice steadied her elbow on the table and chopped her left arm just below the joint. She wrapped the freshly bleeding nub in a paper towel, and handed it to Mrs. Greely. The elderly woman took a bite without hesitation, wiping the blood off her mouth with the back of her hand.

"There's a lot of blood on that one," John said.

"Gross," Mary said.

The front door opened, no doorbell or knock, and Janice's father came in. He didn't shut the door behind him. He carried a chair from the kitchen and sat down next to his wife. Janice eyed her mother's plate. She had in fact not saved anything for her father. Janice cut her arm off at the shoulder, picked it up off the floor where it had landed, and passed it to her father, who took it in two hands. Her father looked around for a larger plate and sighed when there wasn't one to be found.

Janice leaned back in her seat for a moment, wiping her one hand on her dress.

Everyone at the table chewed their meat, smiled at each other, shared bites of the sweet parts, traded favorites for favorites.

Footsteps coming up the porch caught Janice's attention. Her father hadn't shut the door, and she'd forgotten to do it (even if she could). She needed to remember to shut it. Really, to lock it.

A man stood at the threshold. Janice recognized him as the homeless man that lingered at the gas station. Behind him came Marty's ex-wife. Behind her was John's best friend's mother. The three walked in, and no one shut the door behind them.

Gary chewed his food, unconcerned about the door.

Janice cut off her right foot.

The conversation at the table was lively. Where was the homeless man from originally? Marty's ex-wife had gotten a new job. John's best friend's mother was reading a delightful book for her book club.

She started the saw, and she couldn't hear if the discussion continued.

Janice's right leg rolled to the floor. She sawed it at the knee, and put the hunks on the table. Gary stood and carved the leg chunks into smaller pieces, serving each of them in kind. John held the thigh to his mouth, plenty of meat left, so held up his hand when his dad offered him a slice of calf.

The pastor of their church knocked on the door frame as he made his way in and to the table. "You have some of that to go, I imagine."

A woman had followed him in and now stood by his side.

Noticing her, he said, "Welcome, I'm Pastor Hayden." He reached out his hand.

"Crystal," the woman said, politely enough, keeping her own hands on her purse strap. She turned to Janice. "Truly, you're the most selfish woman I know. Here I am again, and you've got nothing left." She swept her hands through the air. "Nothing."

Janice looked down at her pelvis, legs gone. Left arm gone.

"Jan," Gary said, mouth full. "You gonna say something to this broad?"

Janice only had her right hand and arm. She needed those to serve dinner.

"You always have an excuse," Crystal continued. "No one can count on you."

Janice eyed her family. They didn't nod or agree, but neither did they protest. They just ate.

Janice opened the toolbox drawer and took out the filet knife her husband used to clean the trout. Both of her ears came off in one slice each.

Her friend snagged an ear from Janice and marched out of the house. The pastor watched her go, then turned back to wait for Janice, his hands on his hips.

Janice put the second ear on the table and used the sheers for her tongue. She scooped out her left eye with a spoon.

Gary took the tongue and eye, picked up the ear, and put them on a paper towel. He grabbed the three left-over toes from the homeless man's plate for good measure. He balled up the paper towel and handed it to the pastor. The pastor walked out the door and down the porch steps, brushing by another man.

"Knock, knock," the man said. "Should I leave this here?" He held out a package.

"What's that?" Gary asked, marching toward the door. "Do I need to sign for this or something?"

"Nope."

"You wanna stay for dinner?" Gary asked.

Janice tried to catch his eye. There wasn't enough of her to go around as it was. But thankfully, the delivery man said, "I see you've got a house full. Thanks though." He waved to the guests around the table and headed down the porch steps.

"I wonder what the hell this is," Gary said as he returned to the table. He grabbed his steak knife and stabbed through the packaging tape, slicing it cleanly from one side of the box to the next. "I don't remember ordering anything." He ripped open the cardboard flaps and peered inside. "Well, I'll be damned, I'd forgotten about this." He laughed and pulled out a small, white box. He tossed it across the table to Janice. "I got it for your birthday!" He laughed again.

Her birthday had been nine weeks ago.

"What'd you get, Mom?" John asked.

"Yeah, what'd we get you?" Mary asked.

Her family and the other guests waited, grinning.

Janice passed around her gift with the blue print. Scalpels. Disposable, Sterile. #10.

Gary stood up and held the package on his lap wide open for everyone to see. "And I got you ten of 'em."

Indeed, Janice saw nine more boxes. One hundred disposable scalpels.

She opened her mouth to speak, but then remembered. She'd already cut out her tongue.

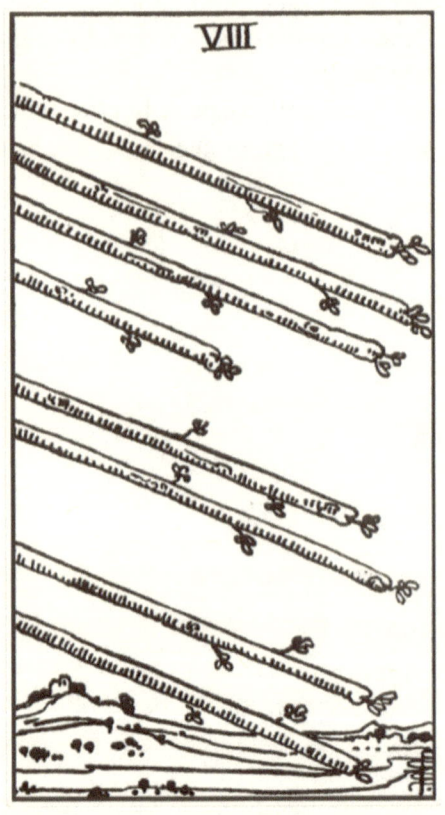

The Brief Aeronauts

~ *Charles Wilkerson*

*The haunted lawn: not be photographed; its full condi-
tion only half-glimpsed, even by the imagination; a hint
of mist; what rises from the bone-broth; a ghost in the
ground; some things eat the grass.*

At the end of a dirt track, always muddy, except for
three days at the height of summer, it's the house you
see first; gray stucco over pale red brickwork that shows
through in patches: grazed flesh and sickening skin. A
wooden door pillaged four centuries ago from a slighted
castle three miles up the road. The curved arch over the
lintel, a later addition, and a pitched roof, slates missing, the worst holes patched with blue tarpaulin. Dia-
mond-paned windows, a few smashed. On the far side,
the lawn stretching out beneath the hill is frayed. Hog-
weed and ferns thrive in the flowerbeds.

All who live in the parish know the house is Hexter
Hall, the name too grandiose for a yeoman's cottage hiding beneath a late Victorian facade. You will not be invited inside, and neither will I. So let's enter with the fumes
from the log fire. A tall thin man who comes from a long
line of tall thin men lies on a sofa. He is coughing, possi-

bly because of the smoke that hangs across the room like lace; but his chest is congenitally weak. Conceivably he was wheezing and spluttering before the match was lit.

On the far side of the room, next to the only window, not so dirty as to exclude rather than admit light, a middle-aged man in a blue blazer sits on a Windsor chair. He brings with him a whiff of sea salt and polished brass. A member of a yacht club, this is what you imagine. I'm unconvinced, for Hexter Hall is far from the coast. The man opens a brown leather briefcase and produces two glossy magazines devoted to aviation and aeronautical matters.

"With our compliments," says the man, whose name you are now told is Justin Buckey. "We're so grateful you've agreed to be interviewed. In addition to your fee you'll be given three complimentary copies of the issue in which our conversation appears."

As he moves to place the magazines on a low table next to the sofa, something invisible touches his face. A soft irritation over the eyes. A spider's web? He brushes it away; then looks at his hand. No silk on the palm.

"You'll stay the night, of course," replies Ned Hexter, not reaching out for a magazine "We're very quiet here as a rule. Imogen will be delighted to have company at supper. Our son's coming back from London. But not till tomorrow."

Hexter is dressed in a dung-beetle-brown corduroy suit and a moleskin waistcoat. His sandals, worn over thick green socks, are propped on the armrest at the far end of the sofa. His head is supported by a threadbare velvet cushion; his long thin face, crowned by white hair that might once have been red, is pale and dominated by the kind of straight nose seen in paintings of medieval monarchs. The mouth beneath: pale rose pink and pursed. I wonder if you've met anyone like Hexter? Justin Buckey has not.

It's humid outside. How many degrees warmer than Hexter Hall, which has no central heating? Not an inkling this afternoon that the lawn is inhabited. We cannot hear the worms underneath or the moan of the trapped ghost. The hedge at the bottom of the garden is rust-brown; killed three years ago by frost. I have a good view of the back of Hexter Hall, one I'm willing to share with you. Most of the stucco has long since fallen off, exposing shoddy brickwork and beams that no one has bothered to paint black. On the ground floor, there is a sash window with several clean panes. The roof tiles are no longer visible beneath the moss. An unstable chimney stack is pointed with nothing stronger than grass. You ask when we can make our way over the weed-riddled lawn and then peer through the window. If we can no longer listen in, at least we can watch them. You follow me as I drift over to the window. The dark brown furniture is too large for the room; the pictures in sumptuously carved and gilded frames must once have hung on far higher walls. They have the merit of concealing the damp. Ned Hexter has risen from the sofa and is warming the back of his long legs by the log fire, which has ceased smoking. Justin Buckey still sits in the Windsor chair. He has been writing in a notebook. What are they talking about? you ask. It is time to inveigle ourselves through a crack in the glass.

Ned Hexter has been speaking mainly of his family history and helicopters, I reply; I thought to spare you the former; much of it is tedious. Now we will hear them plainly.

"I dream of it every night, falling out of the sky in flames," says Hexter.

"There were no survivors."

How could there have been? On impact, it crumpled like an insect. Anyone who hadn't already been asphyxiated or burnt to death would have died as soon as it hit the ground."

"And the helicopter's design?" Buckey begins carefully. "Do you feel . . . well, later some your ideas were adapted with great success."

For a long time, Hexter stares straight ahead. Is he thinking of the men who died or his failure to take out a patent? It is hard to tell, but from our position just inside the room all we can see is the harrowing grief that has condensed his flesh till the skin is taut across his bones. He nods and replies so softly as to be barely audible: "It was a beautiful machine. Beautiful things are often dangerous." He moves away from the fire. "But you must be hungry. I eat very little these days. But there is cake . . . or something . . . in the kitchen. You'll take a cup of tea, at the very least?"

"Yes, tea will be welcome. And whatever else is most convenient."

"I'm afraid that Imogen won't be able to join us. I still have hopes that she may be up to a little supper."

"Your wife. Is she ill?"

Hexter pauses for a moment, as if considering a fine point of law. "Let us say she has changed greatly during these past few months."

"Nor herself?"

"Quite! Now if you'll excuse me."

What you cannot know, and neither Ned nor Justin could be aware of, is that Adrian Hexter, heir to Hexter Hall, its damp rooms, the half-dead lawn and colony of spiders, is at this moment making his way along the road. It will be minutes before he reaches the dirt track. There is no interest in seeing Ned search the cupboards for a cake tin or watching him brew tea in a chipped brown pot; neither is observing Buckey turning the pages of his leather- bound notebook of any significance. From a window over the porch we will witness Adrian's approach.

What should we discuss while we wait? You wish to learn more about Ned Hexter. Why is he living in a ruinous house with no central heating? First, you must understand that none of the Hexters last for long. Note their portraits on the staircase; the line of lineage-proud, short-lived men ascending to the second floor, complete with pictures of their willowy, swan-faced wives. A Hexter would never marry anyone who was not thin and tall. Throughout history most Hexters have, on reaching the age of majority, started well, but few survived long enough to consolidate their achievements. During the infancy and childhood of every succeeding heir, ground was lost: socially, financially - and often literally. The estate has dwindled to the Hall, with its legacy of a haunted lawn.

Ned Hexter talks mostly of helicopters. His family history is a subsidiary interest; he is the longest lived of all the Hexters. He trained as an aeronautical engineer. His ambition, fulfilled with fateful consequences, was to create the most elegant machine ever to take to the air. Whilst capable of carrying a sufficient complement of men to make it a commercial and military proposition, it proved slender, no ungainly pot-bellied troop carrier. Its blades were narrow; almost invisible once airborne. It was perhaps the most silent of helicopters ever designed, rising without undue disturbance, though its thrust and lift were evident as a flattening of grass. I have a photograph of one here. The early model was painted sky blue. Hexter hoped that once sufficient height was gained they would be imperceptible; even on cloudy days seeming no more than a patch of the blue breaking through. He saw them as combining grace, stealth and resilience, as secret as anything made of metal could be in the sky.

But now Adrian Hexter is at the end of the dirt track. Though it is drier than usual, it is still sticky beneath the overhanging beech trees. He moves fluently and at great speed, as if there were not a ridge of dried mud or a pot-hole beneath him; his progress is preternaturally linear. Like his forebears, he is long-limbed. Is he taller than any of them? This is surely not unlikely. You say he seems less substantial. He is wearing a transparent overcoat, somewhat shimmering. An odd way to dress on a balmy afternoon.

We must go downstairs now. The tea has brewed. Ned has found a walnut cake; it sits igneous and dangerously brown in the center of the table. Will the knife be sharp enough to cut it?

The first cup has been poured when the front door is opened and then banged shut. Ned stands heron-like, tea pot in hand. No visitors are expected.

"Who can that be? We are so seldom disturbed at the Hall."

"You mentioned your son ... earlier," Justin reminds him.

"Not expected until tomorrow. It would be most unlike ..."

Then Adrian is in the living-room: a rush of thrashing arms and legs. He's taller than seems strictly conceivably and appears confused. After striking his head on a beam, he sinks into an armchair. His upper body is clad in some kind of waterproof, although the arms are covered by a different material, almost translucent and made of a delicate fabric.

"Well, this is unexpected," Ned remarks. "I'm sure you'd like to see your mother. Unfortunately she's indisposed. We had hopes she would join us for supper, but I suspect that will not now be the case."

"Sorry . . . I'm early. I need to change. That's the problem," said Adrian. His voice is high-pitched yet dry; almost nothing more than a faint squeaking and scraping at a window pane.

"There is nothing to prevent you from changing upstairs. But first I should introduce Justin Buckey. From *Aviation and Aeronautical News*. He's interviewing me."

"Really? I expect to fly soon."

The expression on Buckey's face is one of comprehensive perplexity. He is at a loss to know who or what is addressing him: in English to be sure and the content ordinary enough. But he has never been spoken to in such unfamiliar tones. Finally he manages: "Where to?"

But Adrian has already lost interest. Now it's the orange glow of a lampshade that attracts him.

"Cake, Adrian?" asks Ned. If he is in any way discomfited by his son's appearance and manner, he is disguising it.

"No, thank you, Father. I'm . . . hardly eating at the moment."

"Very well. Perhaps it would be best if you change now. I hope you'll manage a little something for supper."

Adrian has risen unsteadily to his feet; his thin legs look as if they are on the verge of crumpling beneath him. For a moment, he is unsure where to go next. He seems incapable of anything more than imbecilic arm-fluttering. Then he regains control of his body and flickers across the room to the foot of the staircase.

"Now you were asking about the Hexter A6 Helicopter."

"Ah yes," says Buckey, floundering.

"You'll have heard it said that it was a flimsy machine. But the problems were less to do with the design than the materials. The crash was most regrettable, of course."

When Buckey next looks towards the staircase, there's no sign of Adrian. The sounds from above seem almost indefinable, although they could be the old beams settling or a disturbance in the water pipes.

You've seen the photographs and the footage, the machine slowing for a few seconds, suddenly losing height, clipping the top of the canopy on the way down. Then from a different camera, some way off: a view of open fields, the wood in the middle distance. The gray-black smoke rising. Afterwards, the spidery wreckage: the blades twisted, the rest a blackened abdomen. Of course, Hexter refused to accept the blame, although that didn't prevent recriminations and the court case.

In his study, you'll see the designs for the Hexter A6 framed on the wall. And here's an oil painting he commissioned of the A7, flying over the Oxfordshire countryside: as close to being airborne as a machine that never got off the drawing board can be. Hexter believes that his plans were stolen. These box files contain letters from solicitors and counsel. The case went against him. Some thought him unlucky. There hasn't been much to spend on the Hall since then. Lawsuits alleging his intellectual property had been stolen added to the debt. He had to sell what little farmland there was on the estate. He was left with the house and the lawn.

Here's his desk and on the top of it a photograph of Imogen, taken at an air show in the years before the crash. It must have been a cold day for her to wrap up like that. It's only her face that tells you how thin she was. See how the wind has caught her long yellow hair; for a moment, a bright flare on a gray lusterless day. She's in her room now and Adrian's asleep in his. If you listen carefully you can hear Ned cooking supper in the kitchen below. Now it is evening the house is colder. In the living room, Buckey is pacing up and down, plotting tomorrow's early departure. When we slip downstairs, I'm sure that, with Ned out of the room, we'll see him place another log on the fire.

Ned's serving some anonymous meat and thick gray gravy from an orange casserole dish. There's bread in a basket in the middle of the table. Buckey must wonder whether it's warmer in the kitchen. Then he starts. Something small, a moth perhaps, is nibbling at the nape of his neck.

"I'm afraid Imogen is indisposed," says Ned, once he's sitting down. He offers Justin a glass of water. "A pity. She was such an enchanting conversationalist and a great deal better informed about helicopters than one might imagine."

"And your son. What is he reading at university?"

"Aeronautical engineering. Now you may think that is perfectly predictable. But it's become clear that in important respects he takes after his mother."

"Oh!"

"He's started to lose his appetite. I do think it's so important to eat something, don't you agree?"

"Yes," Justin replies, pushing the meat to one side of his plate and toying with the gravy.

"Of course, these days Imogen eats practically nothing. A little honey perhaps."

"What does her doctor say?" asks Justin, as he examines a bread roll.

"Nothing. She hasn't got one."

"Mightn't it be a good idea to . . ."

"No, they're hopeless when it comes to people with Imogen's condition. I've done what I can. Made certain modifications."

"To help her get around the room."

"Yes, I suppose you could say that. She lost a leg the other day."

Hexter speaks of helicopters till late in the evening. Justin is tired by the time they climb the staircase. His host stops to listen at Imogen's door, but there is no sound apart from a noise that might be two of the softest, most fragile things in the world being rubbed together.

From his bed Justin cannot hear Alex in the next room, alighting for a moment on objects, knocking against the walls and then pressing his face to the window pane; for now it is dark, his only desire is to reach the moon.

It's past seven in the morning when Justin makes his way down the staircase. The house is silent. Every piece of furniture seems less itself, as if hiding the potential for use: the table not designed for anything to rest on it, flowers in a vase or a book, but simply an object constructed from wood. He imagines he's first to get up; then through the one good window he spots Ned Hexter on the lawn. He goes out of the back door to join him. It's a fine day, all the more to be valued for being in late summer. The blue above them has the high gloss of a finished product.

A stretch of lawn closest to the pavement is rife with wild flowers and weeds: yarrow, sheep's sorrel, speedwell and coltsfoot. Further on it's studded with plantains smothering the grass. Hexter's standing towards the back, where little flourishes. In spite of the recent rain there are dry, yellowish-brown patches.

"I'll be off soon," says Justin. "I might beat the worst of the rush hour in town."

"Have you seen Adrian?"

"No, not since last night."

"I hope he's up soon. That boy needs to mate."

"Well . . . I think I'd better . . ."

"You're not going yet . . . surely. There's a lot to tell you. After the crash, I went abroad for a year. One of the mothers kept on coming round here. She was quite mad. Making all kinds of accusations. When I returned, the people in the village told me that she'd buried her son's bones right here in the lawn. I've never found them. He was the pilot."

"Do you think he's here . . . beneath us?"

"Not directly. They'll rise soon, but the pilot's ghost won't be with them Although there are days when I know there has been some kind of . . . anyway, you must meet Imogen before you go."

"That's very good of you, but if you don't mind . . ."

"Come on, she'll be most upset if you leave without saying a word."

Hexter's shepherding him back into the house, past the suitcase, which is packed and waiting in the living-room, and up the staircase.

"I'll give Adrian a call first if you don't mind. The window of opportunity is limited. They don't live for very long, the original species." Ned raps on his son's door three times: no reply. "It could happen any time soon. You don't want to miss it." Then turning to Justin: "Incredible! The lassitude of late adolescence."

"Yes, I've one of my own."

Hexter moves on down the corridor and without knocking enters Imogen's room.

"She doesn't seem at her best this morning," he says, signaling to his guest to come in. It takes Justin more than a moment to comprehend precisely what is in front him. The room is empty, apart from a life form he is initially unable to identify. Later he will attribute this to the fact that even the most commonplace creature will be difficult to recognize if magnified perhaps a million times or more. It is evidently an insect of some sort. It has six long legs that appear pencil-line thin in comparison to the mass of the segmented abdomen. The head has compound eyes and antennae, but also a mop of what looks like yellowish-gray human hair. The lips, supple and feminine, are larger than expected, still capable of kissing. The wings are intricate and translucent.

"She lost two of her legs recently. I've replaced them with very fine steel prosthetics. The slightly shinier ones. Do you see? They seem to be holding up well, but one of her own might break off at any minute. So very fragile, alas!"

"I'd better . . . or I'll miss . . ."

"Hold on! Imogen, this is a Mr Buckey. He's something of an authority on helicopters."

The dry sound of a wing brushing against the wall; a metal leg flexing; a pink tongue protrudes—a response?

"Simply must dash. It's been wonderful to . . ."

Then down the stairs and into the living-room. As Justin picks up his suitcase and makes for the front door, he spots Adrian bumping softly against a window pane. Although his waterproof has turned into two wings, his face, refined by inbreeding, is still recognizable. His hair has gone. A full transition appears imminent.

As Justin runs down the drive, his suitcase swinging beside him, a crane fly, its movements marvelously co-ordinated, is swimming through the liquid gleam of late summer air; not clumsy, as it would be inside, but an athlete of the insect world. Within seconds, another has passed him, and then a third. The aeronauts are out to play. Rapturous and long-legged, the crane flies have risen from the lawn. Look how they make love on the wing!

Black eggs in the soil. I have been Hexter, Buckey, Adrian, Imogen, the table, a staircase, a teapot and more besides. I thank you for your time. Let's not wait for winter under the lawn: the pilot's ghost, the leatherjackets feeding on roots. In a dark corner of a room, a ten-day- old crane fly will die, withered by the quest for light, its last flight ending away from the beautiful, dangerous sun.

CONTRIBUTORS

Hermester Barrington

Hermester Barrington is a retired archivist, a haiku poet, and a deliberately genre-ignorant artist whose most recently published ficciones have appeared in *Fate Magazine*, *Mythaxis* and *Tales from the Moonlit Path*. For over four decades, he and his impossibly beautiful wife Fayaway have traveled the round earth's imagined corners in search of lake monsters, spelunking sites, and geomagnetic anomalies.

His latest project is a short film celebrating the protozoans of artificial ponds and streams he collected from miniature golf courses in the United States.

Mary Berman

Mary Berman is a Philadelphia, PA, USA-based writer of science fiction, fantasy, and horror. She earned her MFA in fiction from the University of Mississippi, and her work has been published in Fireside, PseudoPod, Weird Horror, and elsewhere. In her spare time she takes fitness classes and antagonizes her cat.

Find her online at www.mtgberman.com.

Katherine L. P. King

Katherine L.P. King is a horror writer from California. In 2016, she received her MFA in Creative Writing from San Jose State University. Her short fiction has been published in HelloHorror, Coffin Bell, Exoplanet Magazine, Aphotic Realm, and The Sirens Call. When not writing or working at her day job, she can be found whispering secrets to tree blossoms or making candles in her kitchen.

You can find her on Facebook (@katherinelpking).

Gerri Leen

Gerri Leen lives in Northern Virginia and originally hails from Seattle. In addition to being an avid reader, she's passionate about horse racing, tea, and collecting encaustic art and raku pottery. She has work appearing or accepted by *The Magazine of Fantasy and Science Fiction*, *Nature, Strange Horizons, Daily Science Fiction,* and others. She's edited several anthologies for independent presses, is finishing some longer projects, and is a member of SFWA and HWA.

See more at gerrileen.com.

Kimberly Moore

Kimberly Moore is a writer and educator. Her short works are published in *Typehouse Literary Magazine, MacroMicroCosm, Fleas on the Dog, Word Poppy Press*, and *34 Orchard*. She lives in a haunted house where she indulges the whims of cats.

For more information, visit kimberlymooreblog.com.

Erica Sage

Erica Sage is the author of young adult novel *Jacked Up*, published by Sky Pony Press. Her adult short stories have been published by Underland Press and Indie It Press. When she's not reading or writing, she's spending time with her family, hiking, and gardening.

You can find her in the trees or on Instagram (@erica_sage), Twitter (@erica_sage) , and Facebook (@ericasageauthor).

M. Shedric Simpson

M. Shedric Simpson is the familiar of a small black cat. They studied art in Baltimore, MD, before moving to Seattle to live between the mountains and the sea. They spend their free time crafting stories and other small things.

They can be found online at shedric.com or on Twitter (@ink-spiral).

Charles Wilkinson

Charles Wilkinson's publications include *The Pain Tree and Other Stories* (London Magazine Editions, 2000). His stories have been in *Best Short Stories 1990* (Heinemann), *Best English Short Stories 2* (W.W. Norton, USA), *Best British Short Stories* 2015 (Salt), *Confingo, London Magazine* and in genre magazines/ anthologies such as *Black Static, The Dark Lane Anthology, Supernatural Tales, Theaker's Quarterly Fiction, Phantom Drift* (USA), *Bourbon Penn* (USA), *Shadows & Tall Trees* (Canada), *Nightscript* (USA) and *Best Weird Fiction 2015* (Undertow Books, Canada). His anthologies of strange tales and weird fiction, *A Twist in the Eye* (2016), *Splendid in Ash* (2018) and *Mills of Silence* (2021) appeared from Egaeus Press. 2019. Eibonvale Press published his chapbook of weird stories, *The January Estate*, in 2022. He lives in Wales.

More information can be found at his website: charleswilkinsonauthor.com

PAMELA COLMAN SMITH

The tarot images in this issue of Arcana are from the deck illustrated by Pamela Colman Smith. It was released in 1909 as the Rider-Waite deck (so named, at that time, in reference to its publisher, William Rider & Son). It remains the most influential and widely used tarot deck. While the impetus for the deck came from Arthur Edward Waite, Colman Smith was responsible for the iconography of the cards.

Pamela Colman Smith also illustrated over twenty books, wrote two collections of Jamaican folklore, edited two magazines, and ran the Green Sheaf Press, a small press devoted to women writers. She continued to write and illustrate throughout her life.

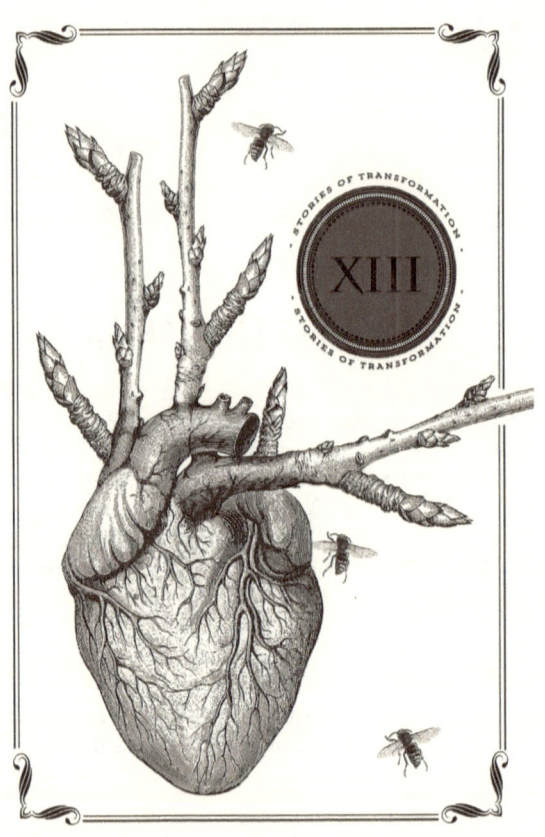

STORIES OF TRANSFORMATION

XIII

STORIES OF TRANSFORMATION

XIII

The thirteenth Tarot card is Death, and he is a symbol not of the end, but of transformation and rebirth. This is the genesis and root of *Thirteen: Stories of Transformation*. The twenty-eight authors of this collection are voices—new and old—who are not afraid to explore what comes next. Whether it be a life after death, a life without love, a life filled with hunger, or the life shared by a ghost. These are stories of the weird, the mythic, the fantastic, the futuristic, the supernatural, and the horrific.

With stories by Liz Argall • M. David Blake • Richard Bowes • George Cotronis • Amanda C. Davis • Julie C. Day • Jetse de Vries • Jennifer Giesbrecht • Daryl Gregory • Rik Hoskin • Rebecca Kuder • Claude Lalumière • Marc Levinthal • Grá Linnaea • Alex Dally MacFarlane • Juli Mallett • Lyn McConchie • Fiona Moore • Gregory L. Norris • Adrienne J. Odasso • Cat Rambo • Andrew Penn Romine • David Tallerman • Tais Teng Richard Thomas • Fran Wilde • A. C. Wise • Christie Yant

Edited by Mark Teppo.

Available at independent bookstores everywhere.

http://www.underlandpress.com

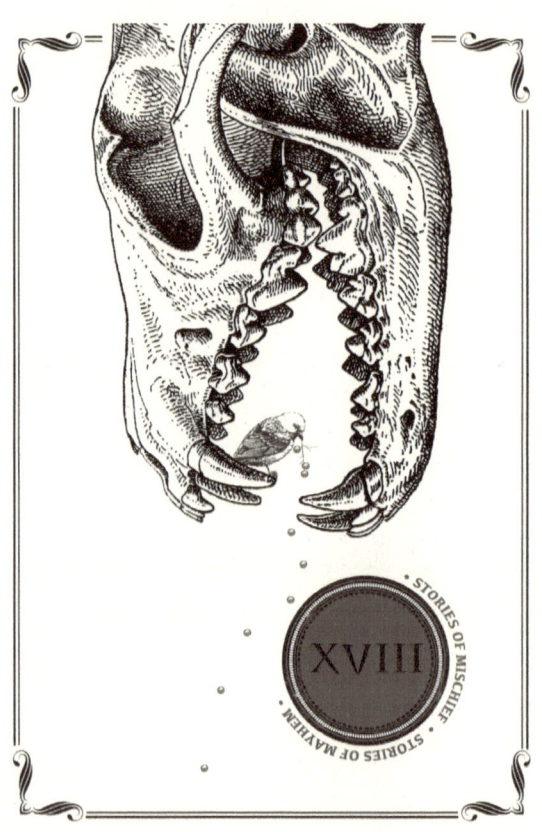

XVIII

• STORIES OF MISCHIEF •
• STORIES OF MAYHEM •

XVIII

The eighteenth Tarot card is the Moon, and those who raise their arms to her know she offers Mercy and Severity in equal measure. This is the great river at night, where wolves howl and all doors are open. All futures are possible, and every truth is elusive. This is the source and passion of *Eighteen: Stories of Mischief & Mayhem*. These twenty-four stories from voices—old and new—celebrate the inevitability of fate, the horror of prophecy, and the shivering delight of not knowing what comes next.

Cross over the threshold with us, and explore the strange, the weird, and the fantastic. Do not fear what lies ahead. It is the same as what came before. The only difference is you. This is *Eighteen*, and nothing will be the same.

With stories by Forrest Aguirre • Darin Bradley • Christopher East • Scott Edelman • Nicole Feldringer • Ben Gamblin • Ingrid Garcia • A. P. Howell • Emma Johnson-Rivard • E. E. King • Jessie Kwak • Shannon Lawrence • Gerri Leen • Mark Mills • Christi Nogle Tammie Painter • Josh Rountree • Erica Sage • Lorraine Schein • J. Dee Stanley • Richard Thomas • John Waterfall • Wendy N. Wagner • Todd Zack

Edited by Mark Teppo.

Available at independent bookstores everywhere.

http://www.underlandpress.com